The Lost Paradigm

Pamela Scotto Tremblay

Donna,
May Joy always
bless your life.

Pamela Tremblay

ISBN: 0-6157-0767-X
ISBN-13: 9780615707679

Library of Congress Control Number: 2012951496
CreateSpace Independent Publishing Platform, North Charleston, South Carolina

Dedication

To my daughter, Trinity, and husband, Mark

may you both seek and experience Joy often.

ACKNOWLEDGEMENTS

I am grateful to God for the dream that created The Lost Paradigm. I am thankful for the support of my family and friends and to my father-in-law, George Tremblay, who spent hours helping me sketch out the details of my first draft. I am indebted to my co-worker, Katie Porter, who took a bare bones manuscript and turned it into a work of art. Furthermore, I appreciate the detail editing work of Dr. Laine Scott. I also value Diane Janusz, Karley Hicks and Jack Slay for doing the final read through of the manuscript.

The flight attendant clears her throat to get the attention of all passengers headed for Dulles, Washington. She tries to talk over their chatter as they find seats, stow luggage, and slam the overhead bins, but she is unsuccessful. She starts again, this time more loudly: "Ladies and gentlemen, may I please have your attention," she says. "The pilot has disappeared. We're unclear if this is a hostage situation, but we're under a Code Red Alert until further information can be gathered."

Some of the passengers stop to listen to the garbled message, but most continue to prepare for takeoff as if nothing was said. A US Marshal with a shaved head, sculpted body, and wire-rimmed glasses stands in the middle of the aisle with a Glock 23 firearm secured on his hip and a five-inch blade strapped underneath his left arm. "Stop what you're doing, now!" he commands.

The standing passengers turn towards the marshal, and everyone else on flight 1212 also pays close attention.

"Secure your belongings, put your children in front of you, and exit through the tailgate on the plane." Chaos erupts in the aisles. In row twelve, seat A, Christine Becker sits with her head propped against her lavender-scented pillow and her ears covered by sound-blocking headphones. A businessman in a dull grey suit nudges her.

"Excuse me," he says. Christine opens her piercing gray-green eyes, framed by honey-brown bangs. "We need to get off the plane." He motions towards the back of the plane.

"What?" She shakes her head.

He stands and grabs his black rollaway suitcase from the overhead bin. "It's a Red Alert. We need to exit the plane." He enters the sea of people moving towards the rear of the plane.

The line moves steadily until it is halted by the sky opening up, unloading buckets of rain onto the unprepared passengers; the women and children scream. "Let's keep it moving, people!" the Marshal bellows down the aisle. "A little rain isn't going to hurt you, but a burning plane will!"

People start moving again, clutching their belongings and pushing those in front of them. The Marshall scolds the passengers again, commanding them to walk swiftly without contact. Christine grabs her luggage and steps into the aisle to exit the plane.

As the rain pelts the large glass windows overlooking the runway at LaGuardia, the passengers at Gate 37 complain about the nasty weather and the disappearance of their pilot. People stand in line to gripe at the gate agents, while others grumble to unknown parties on their cell phones.

Christine Becker, standing five feet, seven inches with a perfect runner's build, begins to pace along the calming pale-blue wall next to the gate. Meticulously dressed in a navy pin-striped suit with matching Ferragamo heels, she grips her phone in one hand and rakes her fingers through her dripping sun-streaked brown hair.

"For God's sakes, Simon, pick up!" she blurts.

Defeated, she tosses the phone into her oversize purse, which holds a wallet with her alphabetized credit cards, an emergency power bar, a Granny Smith apple, and a small makeup bag with pale pink lipstick, concealer and powder. Usually prepared for anything, she waits uncomfortably for the gate agent to reveal the flight's status. The flight representative finally addresses the exasperated crowd, which has waited over an hour since their pilot vanished. The passengers' chatter dies down.

"On behalf of Skyway Airlines, we want to assure you that we're doing everything possible to get you safely to your destination. At this time, your pilot is still missing, and we have been unable to find another one, due to severe weather in New York City, All other connecting flights are completely booked. Unfortunately, we have no alternative but to delay flight 1212 until eight a.m. tomorrow. We will soon pass out vouchers for hotels, and we look forward to serving you then."

"No, this isn't happening to me!" Christine shrieks.

Aware that her car's bald tires cannot make the journey in the rain, Christine takes off running towards the car rental counter at the other end of the airport. Skilled at walking fast in high heel shoes, her suitcase struggles to keep up and begins to wobble behind her on its cheap plastic wheels. From the corner of her eye, she notices the man in the dull grey suit from the plane sprinting behind her. She snatches her luggage by its side handle off the floor and carries it in her arms while racing towards the escalator. As she reaches the bottom floor winded, she is greeted by a host of signs that read *No Cars Available* and a hundred grumbling passengers stranded by rain delayed flights. Defeated, she grabs her phone and hits redial.

Simon, a veteran journalist for *The New York Times*, answers on the first ring. "Let me guess; you need directions to the White House?" He chuckles.

"Not now, Simon. I can't deal with both your sarcasm and my flight being cancelled."

"Your first major White House press conference and you're grounded. What a shame."

"I'll be there, Simon. We're taking off at 7:30 tomorrow morning. I'll make it."

"It will be simply tragic if you don't. I'll have to step in for you."

"Screw you, Simon. Don't give them your name until you hear from me."

"I hope you brought your running shoes. You'll need them to get here on time."

———

Christine arrives at the airport two hours before her departure and unsuccessfully attempts to secure an earlier flight. She wanders into the bathroom, exhausted from lack of sleep because of the scratchy hotel sheets and stiff pillow. Looking into the mirror, she groans, and tries to conceal the fatigue in her face. She takes a deep breath, puts her shoulders back, and heads towards the coffee shop.

She orders a double espresso, a rare indulgence, recognizing that green tea won't cut it today. Walking back towards the gate, she avoids the TV monitors hoping to keep her blood pressure down. She sits patiently, ignoring the screens; however, CNN continues to twist a knife in her side as they report from the outside of the White House where the presidential press conference will take place. She jumps up and paces. Finally, the gate agent announces they are ready to board Flight 1212 to Dulles, Washington.

Christine heads toward the long line of sleep-deprived passengers already at the gate. Relieved to see the on-time status for her flight, she relaxes until the sound of a text grabs her attention. She glances down: It's Simon texting that the Corral doors are open, and he's taking the lead. Christine texts back: *"I will report on the Presidential speech. I appreciate you gathering the preliminary information. I will call you as soon as my flight lands."*

Press Secretary Roberts enters the Corral, the holding room named by the old-school journalist. There is no suggestion of the smile that normally resides on her face as she purposefully closes the doors behind her. Her disheveled hair and dark circles under her eyes belie her composed facade. Roberts clears her throat. As she faces the media, the chatter of voices fades into silence.

"The President will hold a news conference at ten a.m. today in the press room," she begins. "I can't give you any more information now, but we'll have a statement prepared for you later."

A buzz arises in the room. Shouted questions bombard Press Secretary Roberts. "Is the President ill?" "Has there been another foreign attack?" Roberts refuses to comment and slips through the pressroom doors, which block the barrage behind her as they close.

Simon maneuvers through the crowd and out of the room, as reporters murmur in frustration. He strolls to the corner deli three blocks down. After reading the paper and eating most of his breakfast, he takes a final yolk-soaked bite of toast before gathering his briefcase and glasses to head back. He angles through the neophyte journalists filing in the door, desperate to eat something before the press conference begins. Simon then crosses the street to find a quiet corner to call Christine.

"Where the hell are you?"

"I'm almost there," replies Christine, from a rushing taxi.

"If you're taking the lead on this thing, you'd better be here in five or I'm making the call."

"I'll be there, Simon. I'll be there."

With cars bumper to bumper on Pennsylvania Avenue, Christine pays the cabby and sprints towards the White House parking lot on foot. Limos, news trucks, and secret service SUVs snake behind her. Conscious of the situation's severity, she attempts to stifle a smile, realizing that this is no ordinary gathering of key presidential staff. It's not every day that a press conference requires the presence of military personnel, diplomats, senators, and Pentagon officials.

Christine takes the steps two at a time and pauses at the top to straighten her skirt. Sweat gathers at her hairline, forming a perfect bead that trickles down her left temple. She wipes it away and searches in her bag for a notepad and pen. She spots the media signs and follows them back into a cramped hallway, where a host of feverish speculations greet her.

Another 9/11? An assassination? The President is critically ill?

She pushes her way through the crowd of reporters as it barks for a bone, something to take to tomorrow's front page. Relief swells in her as she realizes that she is not too late.

Christine surveys the restless journalists within the cramped quarters as the drone of voices continues to escalate. The veteran media staff among the group, however, appear to be resigned, chatting about vacation plans and rising gas prices. Estimating that there is less than fifteen minutes to go, Christine scans the crowd and searches for Simon in the mass of suits, cameras, and tape recorders. She spots him with a female intern, smiling at the girl and casually brushing against her arm. The only things needed to complete the scene are a martini glass in his hand and a little more leg showing beneath her skirt. Christine elbows her way through the crowd, taps Simon on the shoulder, and smiles.

"Excuse me."

Simon glances over his shoulder at Christine and quickly turns back, only to see the perky, pretty intern walking away. "Perfect timing. I was trying to pump her for the inside scoop."

"Actually, it looked like you were trying to pump her for something else."

Simon sneers.

"I still can't believe what happened to me," Christine rants. "Whoever heard of a pilot disappearing? One moment he's on board the plane and the next he's gone."

"Sorry. I *had* to give them my name. I couldn't risk losing the spot."

"What?" Christine shouts. "I told you I'd make it!"

As if on cue, the doors to the pressroom swing open, and a man begins calling out names from the approved list. Simon's name is called, and the mere sound of it nauseates her. Christine scowls and folds her arms over her chest petulantly. As he walks toward the press room doors, Simon tosses her a quick nod and grins.

"Oh, and Christine? If you were elite status, they would have put you on the next flight." He shrugs. "Better luck next time."

Then, as the doors shut behind him, he disappears.

Christine stands motionless, watching as her dream of being lead reporter dissipates right in front of her. The remaining reporters begin to disperse, lurking in doorways and on the outside steps as they grab a quick smoke, in the hopes of making the time go faster.

The synapses of Christine's mind begin to spark into a wildfire of internal rage; unable to calm herself, she calls Joanne Silverman, her close friend and the one person who can relate to the frustration of working with Simon.

"Do you know what that jackass just did?"

"I take it you're talking about Simon?"

"Who else? He just stole the lead right out from under me." Even as her lips form the words, Christine cannot comprehend their truth.

"How did that happen?"

"I can't even go there. I just need to refocus. Have you heard anything?"

"Nothing but a bulletin about the emergency news conference scrolling across the bottom of the Morning Show."

"I've got to find another angle. Call me if you hear anything."

"What are you going to do?"

"I don't know. Maybe I can find a service worker in one of the corridors, get the story from another angle. Just keep me posted."

"Will do," Joanne replies as they both hang up the phone.

Trying several doors in the now semi-vacant hallway, Christine finds nothing. Desperate, she sneaks into a bathroom stall, sits on the toilet, and holds her knees up in a teetering squat. She waits, hoping to overhear something. When her legs begin to cramp from her awkward balancing act, she reluctantly returns to the Corral with the useless knowledge of a woman's affair with Senator Jones during his family's weekend getaway.

At exactly 9:55 a.m., Press Secretary Roberts again opens the Corral doors so that the rest of the media can enter. She then assumes her position behind the podium with the presidential seal emblazoned on the front.

"The President will make a statement but will not take any questions. I will conduct additional press conferences as needed in the coming hours and days. We appreciate your understanding and cooperation."

"Karma!" Christine exclaims under her breath. "So much for Simon stealing my lead; he won't even get a chance to ask a question." Christine's smile grows wider, and her eyes glisten at the thought.

As Roberts finishes, the doors behind the presidential seal open once again to reveal the President of the United States. His quick gait brings him swiftly to the podium. Following close behind, a number of suits and security come through the same door and line up behind him. "Quite a backup," whispers an anchor standing next to Christine. "Ready for battle, perhaps?" His crew exchanges an array of concerned looks and rolling eyes. Christine recognizes the President's entourage: Vice President Fields, the Secretary of State, the Attorney General, the Directors of the FBI and CIA, the Chief of the Pentagon, and the President's security detail.

With cameras flashing and broadcasting to millions of homes, the President is unable to hide his exhaustion. His graying head hangs on his sagging shoulders, as if weary from the weight. His pale face looks thin and flaccid, his eyes puffy and red. With his brow furrowed in a combination of worry and confusion, he pauses before finally reading a prepared statement from a crumpled piece of paper. His voice betrays him, and he is forced to start again.

"Early yesterday evening, our nine-year-old daughter, Grace, was kidnapped while attending a classmate's private birthday party at the residence of a foreign diplomat. Details are unclear regarding the circumstances of the abduction. However, there is no indication that any particular group is tied to this unspeakable act. While the appropriate agencies are continuing their extensive investigation into Grace's disappearance, I am asking for your help. If anyone can provide any information to assist in bringing our daughter back safely, please contact the Federal Bureau of Investigation. I urge the kidnappers to contact us regarding their demands for the safe and immediate release of our daughter."

With that, his entourage behind him clears a path for the President to make his way to the West Wing door. The room is silent. Stunned faces stare unbelieving at the weary figure leaving the room. For a brief moment the media pauses to share in the fear and uncertainty of a missing child with blonde ringlet curls and bright green eyes, who grew up right before them, but then quickly turn to report it. TV network and cable on-air reporters begin providing their initial comments and questions as to how this could have happened with all the security surrounding the President's family. Christine pauses a moment longer to reflect on the President's pain and then, likewise, begins her personal interpretation.

As cameras focus on the President leaving the press room, the Secretary of State thrusts a note into the President's hand and whispers into his ear. Briefly scanning the note, the President turns and races back to the podium. With a shaking hand and trembling voice, he begins reading. "Your pleas are shallow, and your daughter is an American infidel to be executed like the others." An anguished cry escapes his lips and lingers in the room, penetrating all who are gathered. Forgetting his presidential status, he responds as any father would: "If you harm one hair on my daughter's head, I will find you, and I will kill you. Do you understand me, you sons of bitches!" He slams his fists hard on the podium, sending a screech of feedback throughout the room. He then buries his head in his hands.

As he raises his head, his demeanor changes to one of strength and conviction. Looking into the camera, amid the crowd of people, the President speaks only to his daughter; "Gracie, if you can hear this, stay strong for Daddy. I'm coming to get you!" He tries to blink away the tears from both his anger and his sorrow; as one rolls down his cheek, he wipes it away from his face. The Vice President comes forward and helps him through the West Wing door, where he disappears.

As the doors click shut, they seem to trip an imaginary switch, whirring everything into a frenzied commotion. Cameras continue filming as journalists start talking and texting to affiliates, everyone racing to get their story out first.

Once again elbowing her way out of the room to escape the madness and to gather her thoughts, Christine pulls out her cell phone to call Johnny, her long time friend and source at the Boston Police Department. She scrolls down her contacts to his name but hesitates. Staring at the number, she gnaws on her lip, trying to think of what to say. She's been avoiding his calls for the last several weeks, but, desperate for a different angle, she hits "Send" and waits for an answer on the other end. Johnny answers on the first ring.

"Yes?" He makes no attempt to hide his irritation.

"Hey. How are you?" Christine responds.

"I figured you'd call after the story broke, but I'm not telling you anything."

"Come on," Christine pleads.

"No. How many times have I called you? ... You don't know? Eight. All I get from you is a three-word text: *call you soon*. Eventually, we're gonna have to talk about this, Chris."

"I know. But can we talk about it later? You won't believe the day I've had. I was supposed to have the lead on this thing, but my plane was delayed. *Then* Simon set me up, stole it right out from under me! I wouldn't put it past him to have paid my pilot to disappear."

Trying to listen to dueling conversations, Johnny says, "Hey, can you hold on a sec? I have to see this. We've been messing with the chief all week. He's got Red Sox tickets behind home plate for the last game of the series, tonight."

"How in the world did he score those?"

"His wife won them at the city hall picnic a couple of weeks ago." An exhilarated roar breaks out from Johnny's side, muffling the end of his response.

"What happened?"

Johnny laughs so hard she can hear him gasping for air. "You don't want to know," he finally answers after catching his breath. Christine tries again to pry information out of him.

"Can't you just tell me if you've heard anything about the President's daughter?"

Never being able to ignore her pleas, not since they first met in the second grade, Johnny tries anyway. "So, are we going to talk or what?"

"Yes, I promise," she says.

"Ok, I don't know if it's directly connected to the kidnapping. But here in Boston, we've got multiple missing person reports, and they don't seem to be stopping."

"Really?" Christine jots down several notes. "Maybe my pilot was from Boston," she laughs halfheartedly.

"Hey, Chris, I got to go. The chief's calling a briefing."

"Call me back if you hear anything new," Christine begs.

"How about you call me back when you're ready to talk?" Johnny says firmly.

"I will... just as soon as I finish this story," she promises.

"I've heard that before," Johnny says, then hangs up before Christine has a chance to respond.

Captain Richard Brock gathers his officers in C6, a district station in the Boston Police Department. "Enough pranks already! I'll admit the fake fortune cookie canceling tonight's game was creative, but I need you all to focus. The Police Commissioner sent a personal request: 'The Boston Police Department seeks assistance in locating a 15-year-old male missing from his home in the Beacon Hill area. He was last seen Saturday night at approximately 7:00 p.m. wearing a blue Nike t-shirt, jeans, a blue Red Sox ball cap and white Reebok sneakers. He answers to the name of Tony, but he is autistic and has trouble communicating. Please contact me directly with any information leading to his safe return." The captain blinks at the moisture beginning to gather in his eyes and focuses on the sterile fluorescent lighting hanging from the ceiling. Tony has been a constant in Captain Brock's life since the day he came into this world, the Captain having attended every major life event and Special Olympic race of Tony's. Brock continues, "All missing persons are priority, but keep in mind, Tony is the Police Commissioner's son."

The chief addresses the officers again. "Ok, moving on. Give me an update on last night." One by one, each lieutenant gives a short recap of the night's events, mentioning nothing out of the ordinary until Johnny, Richard's assistant captain, speaks.

"There's been an increasing number of missing person reports. In fact, citywide, there are a total of twenty-two missing persons posted since Saturday afternoon, highlighted right now by the Commissioner's son. A normal weekend averages about four or five postings at most." Johnny pauses, shifting anxiously from one foot to the other. "In addition to the twenty-two, C6 logged twelve phone calls Sunday night from residents reporting missing relatives." Johnny stops talking, leans back against the desk and begins chewing on his thumbnail.

Captain Brock rubs his temples in a circular motion. "Johnny, bring me the details of the website logins from last night." Motioning to the other officers leaning against the wall, "You two follow up on the missing person reports. I have a luncheon at two o'clock, but let's touch base again before I head out for tonight's game. Let's say briefing at four."

Throughout the morning, the switchboard at C6 remains busier than normal. Missing person calls increase rapidly, at times jamming the system. Inside, on-duty officers scramble to keep up with calls from residents, all reporting missing family members. They patiently talk to each person, noting the details and logging them on the virtual site as they conclude. Johnny sticks his head into the captain's office.

"FYI… other BPD districts are posting an abnormal number of missing person reports. What do you think is going on?"

The captain shrugs, "I haven't got a clue."

At four o'clock p.m., Captain Brock returns from the fundraiser luncheon to find his officers waving him into his own office. He walks over to the surrounded computer and takes his seat at the desk. His eyes fix on the computer screen displaying the precinct's website. Unable to comprehend the numbers before him, the Captain's mind travels through possible technical glitches and false reports that could create such numbers. The Website for C6 reports sixty-eight missing persons, and the entire BPD records nearly 250 missing persons, occurring in one day's time.

Captain Brock jumps to his feet and yells, "You guys just don't know when to quit, do you? There are real people missing, including the Commissioner's son, and you think it's funny to file false reports?" He pounds his fists in the air. The mouths of the fellow officers open slightly and their eyes widen as the reddened face of the captain slowly returns to its normal pallor. As if to break the tension, Johnny's figure appears in the doorway. "There's a call for you, Captain. Line four."

Picking up the phone, he politely says, "This is Captain Brock. How can I help you?" He pauses to hear the response from the other end. "You want to fill out a missing person's report. Okay, please go ahead." There's another pause, this time slightly longer. The captain's brow smoothes over and a smirk crosses his lips. "So you're telling me he has brown fur and answers to the name of Captain," he laughs back to those gathered. They have pulled too many stunts today, and this time he is ready for them. He responds, "Might your little fella make a sound like this?" Then, he releases an interpretation of a dog's howl that would make the screech of a fork on porcelain sound comforting. His officers exchange confused looks but, quickly realizing the captain's motives, begin waving arms and exaggeratedly mouthing the word "No." "Hello? ... Hello? ... I guess she hung up." The Captain grins, savoring his victory, as he places the receiver carefully in its cradle.

Almost inaudibly, Johnny whispers, "Um, sir? ... That call was legitimate. She asked to speak with you because she felt that the officer who initially took the call trivialized her dog's disappearance, when he was really trying to keep up with the activity on the C6 Website. And sir, the numbers are accurate."

Mortified, the chief hangs his head. The officers sheepishly slip out of the room, knowing that their mischief over the last two weeks is to blame for the captain's behavior. Johnny steps from the doorway into the office.

"Captain…"

"Out!"

Johnny backs out of the office. In the five years he has known the chief, he has seen him this irritated only once before: when a high-speed chase ended in front of the station and smashed his brand new Mustang. Today, the captain faces a double blow. He lays his head down over his crossed arms, dwelling on the embarrassing phone call and the golden tickets taunting him with padded seats, cold beer, and Ortiz slamming one over the Green Monster.

Brock takes a moment to mourn the loss of possibly one of the best nights of his life, then picks up the phone to relinquish his fourth-row Red Sox tickets behind home plate to his next-door neighbor and son. He cannot ignore it anymore; the situation is real and spreading quickly. Taking a moment to gather his thoughts, Captain Brock massages his forehead before returning the phone to his ear and calling the Commissioner. He braces himself for a long and arduous night, a night in which departments all over the country are being besieged with missing person reports.

———

Christine glances at her watch as she rushes into the subway station; not liking what she sees, she paces until the train pulls into the station and opens its doors for her to board. Too anxious to sit, she squeezes in next to the closest pole for support as the train chugs away from the station's platform. Christine mutters under her breath, "I could walk faster than this," and glances back at her watch.

Ten minutes later, the MTA subway train comes to a grinding halt at 42nd and 8th Avenue. As the door slides open, there is a rush to exit. Caught in the ensuing line exiting through the revolving turn style, Christine shoves her way past twelve other late morning commuters. She throws a quick "sorry" behind her as she squeezes between the metal bar and the front of the line. Despite the apology, the finger pointing and loud swearing continues to follow her as she wedges her way to freedom. Christine climbs the stairs two at a time, reaching daylight and refuge from the crowded train station below. She leans against the railing to catch her breath. Her stomach turns and lurches, and Christine doubles over, clasping her mouth with one hand and supporting her weight with the other. Brushing it off as exhaustion and lack of food, she rights herself and takes another deep, lung-filling breath. Too late to grab something to eat, she hurries towards her destination.

Tall and slender with long, perfectly shaped legs, Christine is beautiful. She commands unsolicited stares from passing men as she quickens her stride in her short, black skirt and high heels. Her weary body attempts to keep up with the pace of her thoughts. Her mind swirls with thoughts of Johnny, Washington, and that jackass Simon. Until that morning, Christine has been consumed with investigating an investment firm whose chairman was indicted for fraud. I need to finish that for tomorrow's edition, she thinks as she steps through the door of *The New York Times*.

Christine's dream has always been to be an award-winning reporter. At Cardinal Spellman High School in Brockton, a blue-collar suburb of Boston, she started her school's first weekly news publication in her sophomore year. By the time she graduated as senior class valedictorian, journalism was her first and only love. With scholarship offers coming from various prestigious colleges and universities, Christine's decision, like many high school graduates, was torn between a local college and a more adventurous location. Gifted in athletics and scholastics, Christine succumbed to the allure of the big city to exert her talents and independence. With a generous scholarship to an even better journalism program, Christine dedicated the next four years studying at Northwestern University.

Her time in Evanston was a blur. She immersed herself in studies, worked as a reporter at the Northwestern student newspaper, *The Wildcat*, but still found time to appreciate the "good times" that nearby Chicago had to offer. She loved the big-city life. With her journalism degree in hand and *magna cum laude* honors, Christine pursued her master's degree and served as a graduate assistant at Northwestern's School of Journalism. Several years and an award-winning story later, Christine secured a position as one of the leading reporters for *The New York Times*.

Late for their weekly staff meeting, Christine bolts from the elevator and through the office. Joanne steps from behind her desk to toss her a Gatorade. "Girl, you don't look so good." With no time to spare, Christine blurts out, "Thanks! …I'll talk to you later," and disappears behind the door to Hal's office.

"It's so nice of you to decide to join us, Ms. Becker," Hal greets her sarcastically.

"I'm sorry, sir…."

"Yeah, yeah, later!" Hal barks. "Now as I was saying, Simon, before Ms. Becker decided to show up, I want you back in Washington right away. Use your inside sources to flush out info about the regime leaders who kidnapped the President's daughter. Also, find out which extremist group claims responsibility and if they are one and the same. Christine, I want you here to investigate any connections between the Washington kidnappings and the pandemic of missing persons."

Christine opens her mouth to object to Simon replacing her in Washington, but instead of words, she feels Gatorade and bile rushing to the top of her throat. Desperately looking for the trash can, she spots it, reaches for it, and just in time, deposits the remaining contents of her stomach into it. Mortified, she runs out of Hal's office towards the ladies' room.

"That's disgusting," she can hear Hal exclaim through the half-opened door, followed by Simon snickering. Joanne waits a few minutes before following behind her into the bathroom, appearing to be the only one in the office genuinely concerned about Christine's peculiar behavior.

Christine and Joanne first met about ten years ago at a small station in Chicago and had actually been rivals trying to move up in the field. Joanne, a couple of years her senior, was assigned as Christine's mentor. She was reluctant to help a newcomer, especially one with the heralded background and academic credentials that Christine possessed. Over time, the two bonded and even teamed up to write several stories. It was the award-winning story they produced together four years ago that gave them national recognition and *The New York Times* simultaneously offering them jobs as investigative reporters.

Joanne opens the door to find Christine at the sink, splashing cold water on her pale face.

"Are you all right?" Joanne asks.

"Yes… I'm fine… really." Christine dabs at her face with a paper towel, trying to regain her composure. "I think I just overdid it this morning on my run."

"When don't you? You're probably just exhausted. You don't think you're getting sick, do you?"

"I wouldn't say 'sick,' just rundown."

"I hope it's just exhaustion. It would suck to be sick with such a killer story on tap. Unless… you're not pregnant, are you?" Joanne jokingly jabs Christine in the arm and waits for Christine to respond, but she receives nothing. "You're not!"

"No. I'm not! I am definitely not pregnant."

"Good, because I'd hate to see you on the sidelines when I receive my Pulitzer Prize," Joanne boasts. "Plus, you saw how a baby slowed me down. Yet at the same time, she's the best prize I could have ever received!"

"I would have to be dead, not just pregnant, for you to beat me to a Pulitzer."

Joanne smiles. "Feeling better already, I see? Look, you should go get something to eat after you smooth things over with Hal."

"Yeah, he's probably pacing the office screaming for a *new* trash can." They both laugh as Joanne exits the restroom.

Christine hangs behind a moment longer to wipe off the weeping mascara around her eyes. She digs deep into her bag, pulling out her makeup kit to reapply some powder. Staring critically at the reflection in the mirror, Christine searches for some inkling as to the unsettled feeling in the dark recesses of her stomach. Finding nothing, she powders her face, dabs on some lipstick, and pops a breath mint. Now looking fresh and composed, she walks back into Hal's office with confidence.

Hal looks up. "What the hell is going on, Chris? What's wrong with you?"

Not even waiting for a response, he continues, "Don't tell me you're pregnant." A look of abhorrence crossed his creviced face.

Twenty years her senior, Hal is a hard man with a chiseled expression. Quick to anger and even quicker to fire, Hal is not a man to be trifled with, but instead requires skillful handling, especially when it came to personal matters.

"Absolutely not, sir. I must have caught a bug or something. It won't happen again."

"Thank God. I couldn't handle a pregnant woman in the office. But if you report me to HR for that, I'll call you a liar to your face."

"Not an issue, sir."

"I need you on your A game. You and Simon have an opportunity to make *The Times* the go-to newspaper people rely on for hard-hitting news covering these disappearances. You've got to stay focused."

Christine nods, focusing most of her attention on breathing through the nausea.

"Delay that indictment story you're working on for a couple of days." He pauses long enough to notice Christine holding her stomach.

"Go home. Get some rest. I've found some interesting angles I want you to explore concerning these disappearances. Let's talk tomorrow."

"I'd really like to try to finish the indictment story for today, sir."

"Home, Chris! You look like crap. We'll run it on Friday."

"O.K..." Feeling too ill to confront Hal about Simon's assignment, she exits his office and gently closes the door behind her.

The revolving doors of *The Times* building deposits the unsettled Christine onto the sidewalk of 8th Avenue. A little slower than before, she meanders toward the subway station in order to return to her apartment in the West Village. On the crowded ride home, the nameless faces and meaningless chatter dissolve as she loses herself to her worried thoughts.

"I can't possibly be pregnant," Christine rationalizes. "What would I do with a baby? I just haven't taken very good care of myself the last couple of days; that's all. I just need to get my act together, focus on this new story. President's daughter; missing people: what's the connection? What am I missing?"

"My period. I've missed my period." A momentary look of panic sweeps across her face. "It's not a big deal," she tries to comfort herself. "It happens all the time. Hectic job, erratic sleep patterns, an exercise addict. Dr. Windsor said this is normal for me. But throwing up in Hal's office! What the hell was that?" Christine's leg jitters as she gnaws on her thumbnail. Searching her mental filing cabinet for answers, she stumbles over an awards ceremony and a reckless Saturday night. "Oh, my God," Christine exclaims, covering her mouth with her hand as the girl dressed in black with multiple facial piercing turns and stares.

As the train pulls away from her station, Christine stands frozen to the platform as people push past and around her motionless body. A misguided elbow to her side jolts her out of her head and back onto the platform. "Sorry," the owner of the elbow offers over his shoulder. Christine merely nods in response and climbs up the stairs into the heat of the afternoon. Looking around, she remembers the drugstore just a block away. With a determined gait, Christine barges through the door and rummages up and down the aisles for a Clearblue Easy.

Snatching the box off the shelf, she heads straight for the counter, shoving the box and her credit card at the unsuspecting clerk.

Impatient, Christine takes her new purchase to the back of the store and into the bathroom. She tears open the package in the bag and throws the box on the floor next to the toilet. In the same moment, Christine yanks her skirt up above her waist and closes the stall door behind her with her shoe. Nearly ripping off her white lace panties while pushing them down to her ankles, she foregoes lining the seat and plunks down onto the toilet. She begins to pee on the small white stick she holds between her legs. As if waiting for a Polaroid to develop, Christine anxiously watches the first blue line appear... and then the second. Panicked, she grabs the second applicator from the box and takes the test again, willing herself to void every necessary drop. Again, two blue lines come into view. Christine slumps forward, hanging her head over her bare knees. "This can't be happening to me," she groans for a second time this week. Christine hears the door open as a pair of heels step into the bathroom. She snatches her underwear from her ankles and slips it over her hips as the clicking heels enter the adjoining stall. Aching to avoid reality waiting on the other side of the stall door, Christine waits to hear the adjacent stall door lock. Devastated, she shoves the evidence into her bag and pulls herself together to face the unavoidable truth. Exiting the store, Christine wanders, deep in thought, up the last two blocks to her apartment.

She enters her building and climbs the three flights of stairs to her apartment. Fumbling for her keys, she loses her grip, sending her handbag tumbling to the ground and spilling the contents, including the two dreaded pregnancy tests. Tears well up in her eyes and then gush forth down her cheeks into the crevices of her mouth. Her body trembles with the sobs that escape her lips as she buries her head in her hands. Hearing footsteps behind her, Christine throws everything back into her bag, unlocks the door, and collapses into the security of her apartment. Bolting the door behind her, Christine falls backward onto the closed door, extracts her phone from her purse, and calls her doctor's office. On the second ring, the familiar voice of Dr. Windsor's receptionist, Patty, answers, "Women's Medical Center." Like molasses, Patty's voice oozes the slow, smooth drawl of Charleston, an odd but comforting anomaly in the sharp bite of the Big Apple.

"Hi, Patty, this is Christine Becker. Can Dr. Windsor's fit me into her schedule this week?"

"Actually, I just had a cancellation for 8:30 tomorrow morning. Does that work?"

"That's perfect; thank you."

"Great. Then we'll see you first thing in the morning."

"Have a good night." Christine hangs up the phone, tosses it onto the hall table next to her keys, and walks into her living room for the first time in three days. At thirty-eight years old, she feels her life slipping and spinning out of control, an endless teacup ride she is unable to get off. Christine collapses onto the sofa, grabs the remote, and clicks on the TV to Brian Williams reporting on the disappearance of the president's daughter and the thousands of alleged missing people. Her journalistic mind is briefly triggered but then drifts to the two thin blue lines on the stick. In an effort to quiet her racing mind, Christine flips through the remaining 199 channels, finding nothing but infomercials and reruns. She presses "off" and throws the remote on the coffee table.

Worn from the stresses of the day and the worries of her mind, Christine heads to the bathroom, unbuttoning her blouse as she goes. With a trail of discarded clothes behind her, Christine steps into a hot shower, a futile effort to wash away the barrage of thoughts in her head. After brushing her teeth and combing the knots from her long brown hair, Christine stands before the mirror, inspecting her naked body, but she can find only her usual fit frame reflecting back. Resolved, she throws on a heavy, white spa robe that Joanne gave her for her last birthday.

Walking through the living room, she unlocks and climbs through her window. She steadies herself, steps onto the fire escape, and heads up to the rooftop, where she has secretly created her own personal sanctuary. She ties her robe, lies down in the upright chaise lounge and covers her legs with a small blanket. Aching to relieve the anxiety she feels, Christine closes her eyes and focuses on the long deep breaths filling her lungs and calming her body.

Christine's mind wanders aimlessly to that reckless yet wonderful Saturday night at the Waldorf Astoria six weeks earlier: *The New York Times* annual banquet honoring outstanding reporting, which was the highlight of the year for all employees, even upper management.

Nearly five hundred guests had attended the dinner, the majority in tuxedos and festive evening gowns. At the cocktail party earlier, Christine had sipped a glass of chardonnay, watching the festivities unfold. She could still taste the wine as it slipped down her throat, warming her inner core. It was a special occasion after all; she would just run an extra mile in the morning. She splurged on the scrumptious filet mignon dinner with abundant Cabernet Sauvignon from Sonoma County. As she walked back from the restroom to join her date, Christine's stunning off-white, floor-length Chanel dress clung perfectly to her flawless body, which she accentuated with just the right bling dangling from her ears. Joanne had convinced Christine to buy the dress just a couple of weeks earlier, claiming that she needed to make a statement at tonight's gala. Eyes followed Christine as she ambled back to her table to join her date and the remaining party of eight: Hal and his wife, Joanne and her husband, and Simon and his current flavor of the month.

Ten awards were presented that night, and when it came to announcing *The New York Times* Outstanding Reporter of the Year, the only surprised faces in the room were Christine's and, of course, Simon's. At the sound of her name, *The New York Times*, arguably the most prominent newspaper in the world, had recognized all of Christine's drive, talent, and diligence. All eyes in the extravagant ballroom were fixed on Christine as she gracefully made her way to the stage to receive her well-deserved award. She accepted the award and stumbled over her unrehearsed words, thanking Hal, her fellow reporters, and specifically Johnny for having served as her sounding board and support all these years.

Johnny was her escort that night. Having few dates since her arrival in New York, Christine focused on her career and avoided cultivating a serious relationship. With the awards banquet approaching, Christine did not want to be dateless, as she had been the year before. In a last-ditch effort, she called Johnny a couple weeks earlier and asked if he'd come down to the city to be her escort. Her childhood friend for over thirty years, Johnny could never turn Christine down. He enthusiastically accepted and looked forward to seeing Christine, even if it meant he would have to rent and wear a penguin suit — something he despised, yet had done before, the first time being when he took her to the prom.

Returning to her seat, Christine was bombarded with handshakes and hugs from her dinner party and from nearby tables. She could barely hear the master of ceremonies announce the thanks-for-coming-drive-safely speech. After a quick snapshot of all the winners on stage with their plaques, everyone broke to the bar for after-dinner drinks. Christine could not erase the silly grin on her face or the dazed look in her eyes, a combined result of the win and the wine. A toast to the winners and three glasses later, Christine hung on Johnny's arm and whispered in his ear, "Hey...You're so... handsome." Laying her head against his shoulder, she looked up at him and grinned. Taking her wine glass from her hand and placing it on the bar, Johnny responded "O.k., princess, I think it's time for someone to call it a night."

The approaching whirr of sirens interrupts Christine's reverie. Looking over the brick wall protecting her from the depths below, Christine sees three squad cars pulling into the intersection. One officer ejects from his car and darts around the corner, while the remaining two disappear into a nearby tavern, chasing what appeared to be a homeless man. That's odd, she thinks. In the past two years, Christine witnessed action like this only once before, and that turned out to be a false lead made by an angry property owner three buildings down.

After a few passing moments, the officers reappear and climb back into their squad cars with the tattered clothed man in handcuffs, silence the sirens and flashing lights, and then fade into the city night. Quiet once again descends on the neighborhood, leaving Christine wondering whether it even happened at all. Settling back into her chair, she gazes at the cotton-candy clouds wafting across the sky and once again allows her mind to drift.

Johnny and Christine had lived on the same block in Brockton, and, together, they had learned the alphabet and studied times tables in the second-grade wing of the elementary school, with a mural of children with gigantic heads painted on the wall. Their families were close, and with her dad's passing shortly after her sixth birthday, Christine's friendship with Johnny only strengthened. After school they would kick the soccer ball in the front yard and ride bikes around the block. One summer night, Christine and Johnny were racing each other around the neighborhood as the darkening sky chased the setting sun. As they turned the corner, the front tire of Christine's new pink Huffy bike caught a rock, sending her crashing over the handlebars and into the curb. Bracing herself for the fall, Christine skinned up her knee and the palms of her hands. Seeing Christine in tears, Johnny slung her small arm over his shoulder and carried her home, returning later with the bike.

After that summer, things changed... but not really. Johnny's dad's promotion moved him across town into a better neighborhood and a rival high school, where he quickly adjusted into the starring role of varsity quarterback. Christine and Johnny remained close friends, supporting each other through heartaches and disappointments and keeping each other's deepest secrets. Romance was never a question; risking the loss of such a companion for the mere inkling of a kiss? Christine would rather waste her affection on emotionally unavailable men.

After graduation, they called each other once a week and sent birthday cards once a year. Every Sunday night at eight o'clock, Johnny would call to discuss their current flings, their current assignments, and their current complaints. Never venturing beyond the Massachusetts state line, Johnny accepted a football scholarship to Northeastern University in Boston. Life was good until his junior year. With five minutes left in the fourth quarter, Johnny snapped the ball and was tackled from the right, twisting his knee and tearing his ACL. The fourth-quarter buzzer signaled the end of the game and Johnny's football career. He majored in business, married a college sweetheart at twenty-five, moved to Marshfield, and divorced four years later. After suffering through a short career as a CPA, Johnny left his lackluster job and marriage and moved back to Boston to join a few close buddies as a member of the Boston Police Department. Johnny was now happy and fulfilled in his new position as the chief's assistant.

The gathering at the Waldorf Astoria bar was dwindling as the hour hand slid toward two. Management at *The Times* knew the tendency of their employees to overindulge on this special occasion, so it had become customary for them to book rooms at the hotel for its dinner attendees. It was a small price to pay to reward excellent work and avoid a lawsuit.

Johnny encouraged Christine to say her final goodbyes for the evening. "See you bright and early on Monday," Hal called after her as Johnny, hand delicately placed on the small of her back, led her swaying body out of the bar and toward her room. He guided Christine into the elevator, and pushed the fifth floor button. The elevator jerked into motion, sending Christine into Johnny's arms. She snuggled once again into his embrace, looking up to peer into his familiar eyes.

"Your eyes are green," Christine whispered.

"And your eyes are brown."

"That's right...I'm your brown-eyed girl." Christine smiled her drunken smile, unusually droopy on one side, and slid her arms up his chest and behind his neck. As she leaned in a little closer, the elevator dinged and the doors slid open, revealing the fifth floor lobby.

"Saved by the bell," Johnny laughed as Christine stepped away, and he slid his arm over the door, holding it open. Christine exited first and Johnny, although staying on the seventh floor, got off the elevator to walk Christine to her room.

At her hotel room door, an observer would have presumed that the overly dressed couple, fumbling for a room key, suffered from end-of-the-night first-date jitters. But there was no one to observe as Christine located the room key, slid it in the door and turned to embrace Johnny.

"Thank you… for coming all this way to be my date tonight," she whispered into his ear. "I don't know what I would do without you." Christine momentarily pulled away then leaned in again to kiss him on the cheek. Unknowingly, Johnny turned, finding her lips intertwined with his. Thirty years in the making, their first kiss on the lips awakened an unknown feeling deep in the bottom corner of Johnny's heart.

Overwhelmed by this unearthing, Johnny jerked away, drawing his hand up to his lips. "I can't do this, Chris – not when you've been drinking."

Christine, unembarrassed, raised her piercing gray green eyes to meet his and, aided by the wine, freed herself to speak: "But I need you … I've always needed you."

With the utterance of these words, their fate was sealed, for Johnny could never deny her anything, and Christine was five sips past tipsy. Although Johnny's mind pleaded to leave, to avoid the inevitable heartbreak that would surely follow, his heart, encouraged by his lower regions, longed to stay with her. Johnny nodded, agreeing to her plea, and Christine pulled him toward her and into her room. Without pretense or false modesty, Christine stripped Johnny of his rented jacket and trousers, then made quick work of his crisp shirt. Johnny slid his hand down her back, located the zipper, and began to peel her dress slowly from her body. Naked, they fell unencumbered into the bed.

A meek voice whispered for her to stop, to elude a wine-induced mistake, but the warmth of Johnny's bare body created a security in which she drowned and passed into a newly discovered world of passion. His gentle touch and sensual kisses quieted the brief chatter distracting her mind. Christine succumbed to a place she had never known existed, a place where the earth conspired to still time, allowing her to absorb each moment, each movement, until she lost herself in an act from which there was no turning back. There was no returning from the fierce passion they shared, as Johnny made love to her the first, second, and final time. With her hair drenched in sweat and her body trembling, she found refuge in the crook of his arm and fell into a long, deep, peaceful sleep.

A tinge of pink flushes Christine's cheeks as the memories evoke a joy that she has purposely avoided: a better-forgotten evening that would now influence her life in ways she couldn't even imagine. Resting beneath her favorite blanket, Christine stares into the dark sky, searching the universe for answers. Had the alcohol lured her into reckless behavior, or did it only open her heart to what had been there all along? "Why is this happening?" she questions aloud. "How could I let this happen? This is exactly what I always wanted to avoid with him." And then the fear sets in. "You idiot! You can never get back what you had together." Like a wave creeping up the beach on an incoming tide, she realizes that Johnny can never know. Pregnant or not, Christine knows that the outcome will be the same. She will never be a mom, so how could she tell him he was almost a father? Overcome with helplessness, Christine crawls back down the ladder, into her apartment, and slips into bed, emotionally exhausted.

At 8:26 a.m., Christine paces outside the glass doors of the Women's Medical Center. Patty sashays her large Southern hips over to the locked door and turns the key, allowing Christine to enter the waiting room.

"Please have a seat, Christine. Dr. Windsor will be with you in just a few minutes." Patty's usually soothing drawl irritates her. Christine nods as she plops down in an uncomfortable chair, picks up a magazine, and absently thumbs through the pages. As Christine reaches to exchange one magazine for another, her name is called from a door on the other side of the room. She grabs her oversized bag and rushes over to the now-open door. The nurse checks her chart, as she ushers Christine into the examination room. "Dr. Windsor will be right with you" she smiles, as she shuts the door behind her. Christine climbs up onto the examination table, dangling her legs as she waits. A small eternity later, Dr. Laura Windsor opens the door and steps in.

"Good morning, Christine."

Before Dr. Windsor can say more, Christine blurts out, "I think I'm pregnant. I took these yesterday." She shoves the two positive pregnancy tests in the doctor's direction. "Can they be wrong?"

"Well, it's rare that both would be wrong, but let's not speculate. We'll do a blood test."

"But that will take days! Isn't there another way?"

"We can do another urine test in addition to the blood test," Dr. Windsor says in her most comforting tone. "If you get another positive result, chances are you're pregnant."

"Let's do them both then."

After being prodded by needles and urinating in a small plastic cup, Christine sits alone in the sterile room surrounded by diagrams of the female reproductive system and the 40-week development of a growing fetus. Christine feels yesterday's anxiety seeping up into her racing heart.

"I just can't be pregnant," she says aloud. "I can't."

The door opens and Dr. Windsor comes in, smiling broadly, and announces, "Congratulations, dear Christine — you're going to be a mommy after all."

"Are you positive?"

"99%. But we'll know for sure when we get the results back." Christine's face falls, devastation flooding into and weighing down every pore. Dr. Windsor musters the only comfort she can provide: "Listen, Christine, you're not alone in feeling that there is never a perfect time to have a baby. But you've always told me you wanted a baby, and now your wish is coming true."

"Just stop, please." Christine shakes her head, attempting to keep the doctor's words from reaching her ears. "I don't want to have this baby! I won't have this baby."

"I don't understand." Dr. Windsor sits down in the vacant chair designated for purses, coats, and fathers-to-be. "I've been your doctor for almost eight years since you've been in New York." Again, she pauses, seeking the right words to calm Christine's mind. "We've even talked about freezing your eggs in case you wanted to explore motherhood. So look at it this way. Hopefully, it was a lot more enjoyable, right? And cheaper?"

Christine hops down from the examination table and begins to pace, glancing at the floor to avoid the taunting images of developing babies. "I know I said I might want a baby some day, but that was years ago. Things have changed. My career, my life, I...I can't give that up for changing dirty diapers and washing bottles." Tears begin to stream in a constant flow down Christine's face as the reality of it all plows over her like an offensive line reaching for the fifty. Dr. Windsor awkwardly pats her on her heaving shoulders in a failed attempt to calm her. She can feel her silent sobs, a panicked pain that's inaudible to the ear. "Everything will be all right," Dr. Windsor soothes. "You just need some time to think."

"Stop — you don't understand!" Rejecting Dr. Windsor's less-than-comforting words, Christine pleads, "I need you to terminate this pregnancy!" A look of determination lights on her face.

Dr. Windsor returns to Christine's file and begins to write with a renewed urgency.

"Do you hear me? I need you to terminate this pregnancy."

"I hear you," Dr. Windsor states. "I hear someone who is in shock and acting impulsively because she's scared."

"Yeah, I'm scared! I can't go around puking in my boss's trash can like I did yesterday! I can't be a prized reporter, be effective in my job carrying a baby on my hip. I don't want this baby."

Reflecting on Christine's words and choosing her own words even more carefully, Dr. Windsor responds. "Christine, I will perform this abortion, but only after you have thoroughly deliberated on what you are asking me to do. I've seen too many women plagued by the guilt and regret of having an abortion, without thinking through all the ramifications."

"What are you saying?"

"I want you to talk with someone as soon as you can arrange it. Here's his card." Dr. Windsor flips through a display of business cards and pulls one out to hand to Christine. "Once you sign the consent form that Patty will give you, I will call him with a brief history. When was your last period?"

"About two months ago. You know I've never been regular. But about six weeks ago, I drank too much wine, slept with my best friend and now I'm here in your office, trying to fix the biggest mistake of my life."

"Everything will work out, Christine. We have some time here. Meet with Dr. Abba. Once he feels certain that you're making a conscious decision, he'll advise me whether a surgery is needed at that point."

"Fine! I'll meet with him today. Can we go ahead and schedule the procedure for tomorrow afternoon?" Christine wipes her face with the back of her hand, and grabs her bag to leave.

"Christine, he's very busy. It's doubtful that you will get in to see him this week."

Christine stops to face Dr. Windsor, disbelief on her face.

Dr. Windsor ignores her evident frustration. "When you call his receptionist for the appointment, make sure to tell her that I referred you and it's of critical importance that you see him as soon as possible."

"Fine... I'll do this, but I'm telling you now, I am not going to change my mind."

As the alarm clock sounds, Kate opens her eyes, then closes them in disappointment. She sighs at the empty space lying next to her, the space where her husband should have been. Irritated, she sits up and leans over, slamming her hand down on the annoying sound of the alarm clock and silencing it. Kate rubs her face and eyes in a rapid motion, willing herself awake as she slips on her robe and puts on her glasses. Running her fingers through her hair to calm the usual bed-head, she walks down the hallway towards the living room, and yet another letdown.

Kevin's massive form lies unresponsive on their hand-me-down couch. The coffee table is littered with empty beer bottles, and fast food wrappers are scattered all over the floor. The television static pierces her ears as she fumbles through the wasteland for the remote. Unable to find it in the mess, she stomps over to the TV to press "off." She turns to face the now daily sight of his hung-over body draped grotesquely on the couch. She approaches him, stepping over last night's binge, and forcefully kicks his feet off the couch. Startled and confused, Kevin sits up and rubs his eyes.

"Was I snoring?" Kevin tries to focus on the angry vision of his wife.

"How would I know? We don't sleep in the same bed anymore."

"I'm sorry, Kate," Kevin whispers.

"I know, Kevin, but it's the same story night after night. When is this ever going to end?" In an attempt to calm her, Kevin replies, "It will. I promise."

"Sure, it will." Kate nods before walking back into their bedroom to get ready for work.

Kate slams the bathroom door behind her, hoping that Kevin's aching head will suffer for it. Standing in front of the pedestal sink, she pounds her fist against the porcelain top and grimaces in pain. She gazes up at the mirror above the sink and comes face to face with the deep sorrow in her eyes projecting back at her. Kate sobs. Finding it increasingly difficult to shoulder the burden of Kevin's excessive drinking, Kate senses that her patience and compassion are waning. The one person she longs to confide in is the one person she cannot reach.

As she showers and dries her short blonde hair, Kate's thoughts wander along the uncharted path of her future. For the past two years, she has endured the challenges of Kevin's condition, the helplessness she feels after every futile attempt to aid in his recovery. She would be the first to admit that things haven't always been good between them, but her love for Kevin has never wavered during their brief courtship and seven-year marriage.

As if by fate, Kevin and Kate met at Utica College in upstate New York on the first day of their freshman year. His rugged good looks were a magnet, pulling her as the moon pulls the tide. Her eyes could see right through him, exposing him in a way he had never before experienced. Their immediate romance revealed a kindness, a passion that united them long before the need for a priest. Reckless and seeing no reason to postpone the inevitable, they married after their junior year, much to the chagrin and disapproval of Kate's parents.

They struggled together through their senior year, living on love and ramen noodles in their tiny studio apartment a couple of blocks from campus. Building their married life together was all that mattered. After graduation, Kate was fortunate to be recruited by numerous firms and was quickly hired on as a financial analyst for a prominent Wall Street brokerage firm. Kevin, however, struggled with the lack of financial means to pursue his dream of becoming a veterinarian, and while their money was a joint possession, he blamed himself for their quick marriage and lackluster life. Without discussion, Kevin had enlisted in the Army Reserves, enabling him to pursue his veterinarian degree at NYU.

Kate had always had the finer things: a Lexus instead of a Honda, a weekend in the Hamptons instead of a weekend at the Hampton Inn; but she had never said a word to Kevin about her downgrade to "common." She deserved the finer things, and Kevin's drive and ambition would see that she got them. In that dark place of her heart, Kate knew that he would never let her support him through veterinary school. So, despite her anger for his failure to consult her in his choice to enlist, Kate had finally accepted the reality of the commitment he had made.

Hearing Kate's sobs through the paper-thin walls of their apartment, Kevin slumps with the sadness that has invaded their marriage. Unable to deal with the bright light of the morning sun and the stress of their dying relationship, Kevin places a pillow over his head and lies back down on the couch to escape the pain. Dressed and ready for work, Kate reappears in the living room and discovers Kevin still on the couch. She once again kicks his feet off the couch, causing him to suffer a sharp pain in his head as his body is propelled upward.

"Now what?" The fighting words are muffled through the pillow.

"If you are going to miss school again, the least you can do is clean up this sty and fix the leak in the bathroom."

"Ok, Kate," he mumbles.

Annoyance dominating her voice, Kate refutes, "You've told me that for the last two weeks. I just don't know how much more of this I can take!"

"I know," Kevin groans, slipping back down on the couch.

His all-too-predictable response angers Kate, and she slams the door as she leaves the apartment. Leaning against the entryway to her home, she breathes in deeply, trying to blink away the tears. She then rises to her full height and walks the ten steps to her neighbor's door.

A few months earlier, Kate had met her new neighbor, Jesse, at the quarterly tenant meeting. Of course, Kevin hadn't come. It would have interfered with his new love, Jack Daniels. They talked about the building issues, their families, and their jobs, really making a connection. Kate hadn't experienced that level of conversation with another man since Kevin came back a stranger.

Kate, intrigued by Jesse's background as a certified therapist, has found herself standing on his doorstep on more than one occasion since. Today, she musters up the courage again to knock.

Through the peephole, Jesse recognizes the figure of his next-door neighbor, ready to punch numbers for eight hours of pay. He notices her puffy red face, the aftermath of slamming doors and tears. He swings open the door. "Hi, Kate."

"I'm sorry that I am here so early. I was making breakfast and realized I didn't have enough sugar. Could I borrow a cup?" Kate stammers through the counterfeit request.

"Sure," he smiles. "Come on in, Kate."

As Kate steps through the door into his homey but sparse apartment, the thin veneer of her composure comes unglued. "I know the last thing you need is to hear about someone else's problems, but I have no place else to turn."

Jesse closes the door behind her. "Have a seat. How about some coffee?"

"Thanks, but no thanks, Jesse. I think caffeine is the last thing I need right now." Kate attempts a smile. "I just can't take it anymore. Kevin's drinking is out of control. I don't even know who he is anymore. I can't find a trace of the man I fell in love with. He has to be there, but I don't know how to reach him anymore. He doesn't go to class, he has no ambition, and we don't even sleep in the same bed anymore." She stops, embarrassed for revealing so much and then starts to back track. "I don't want to leave him, but I can't keep living like this, either. I want my husband back. What do I do?"

Jesse's rubs his forehead as he contemplates her words, the cry for help of a desperate woman standing in the middle of a forking road. "You need to go see a marriage counselor, Kate. Together."

"He got mad when I suggested it, says he knows what the problem is and doesn't need to pay a shrink to tell him the obvious. But he's not doing anything on his own to fix it. We've got to make a change, or we're going to end up hating each other."

Kate glances at her watch. "Oh, I'll miss the train. I appreciate you letting me barge in like this, really." She reaches for the knob and opens the door.

"Hey, I'll get you the sugar, Kate." She halfway turns in the doorway, leaning against the open door. A slight smile betrays her appreciation for his playing along.

"Thanks, Jesse." She closes the door behind her.

Feeling frazzled as she leaves Dr. Windsor's office, Christine breathes in the morning light before ducking into the dark garage to retrieve her car. In the early morning, the city looks its best to Christine. It's when everything appears clean and fresh, before the heat of the day burns off the dewy glow to reveal the dirt and grime beneath. The street vendor smokes his third cigarette of the morning as he counts change for hurried suits buying newspapers, heading to Wall Street. The early aroma of fresh bagels wafts through an open door of the bakery on the corner as eager birds chirp while waiting in the nearby tree for crumbs. This is her favorite time of day, usually enjoying the simple things in life during her early morning run. But this morning is just like any other time of the day, and Christine is on assignment, a personal assignment. She opens her car door, gets behind the wheel, and fumbles for her phone and a twenty to pay the attendant.

"Dr. Abba's office. How may I help you?" The receptionist's voice is mechanical. A horn honks, returning Christine's focus to the road. Back in her lane, she answers.

"Yes, my name is Christine Becker, and I would like to make an appointment with Dr. Abba. This week, if possible." Christine grips the steering wheel of her car and yanks it into the next lane as the cabbies play chicken with each other. I hate driving in this city, she mumbles to herself, frustrated that her tight schedule has dictated that she must drive to the office this morning.

"I am sorry. That's not possible. Dr. Abba is booked all week. Let me look for his next available appointment."

"Excuse me?"

"It's not possible to see him this week. His next available appointment is on the 19th."

"In two weeks?"

"No. Two months from now."

"What?" Christine shrieks. "I don't think you ..." Christine's focus is yanked to the approaching red light. Pressing the brake pedal as hard as she can, she braces herself for impact, but none comes. Breezing through the red light, she doesn't breathe until she finds herself safely on the other side. Her body pulses with adrenaline, encouraged by the ceaseless honking of surrounding cars. A taxi driver finishing his shift freely expresses his frustration, waving his middle finger at her as she drives past.

Christine slowly fills her lungs with air. Some people.

"Hello? Are you there?" The robotic voice calls from the cell phone now lying in her lap.

"Yes. I'm here. As I was saying, I don't think you understand the situation here. I don't have two months. Dr. Windsor insisted that I meet with Dr. Abba as soon as possible. I am not in a good place right now, and it is critical that I see him."

"Dr. Windsor referred you?" Christine could hear a slight change in her mechanical voice, turning it almost human with concern, as if certain gears have clicked into place in her mind to reveal the true need for the appointment. "Let me see what I can do."

Thank you. Christine whispers in to the air, not really caring if the receptionist hears her or not.

"Let's see... I can squeeze you in at 8:30 for thirty minutes two weeks from Thursday. That's the best I can do."

"Fine, I'll take it."

Pulling up to a red light, Christine brings the phone from her ear to dial Dr. Windsor's number. As her car slows to a stop two inches over the pedestrian line, a small-framed girl with short blond hair slams her hand on the hood of Christine's car.

"Watch where you're going, lady," the girl shouts at her through the windshield. The glare on the glass makes her image appear much younger than her true age. A gentle face forced to live a less than gentle life. The slump in her shoulders carries the weight of the world, as if Atlas grew tired and asked her to take over for a while.

The light turns green as the slow drawl of Dr. Windsor's receptionist answers the call.

"Yes, this is Christine Becker. I just left the office a little while ago. I have an appointment to meet with Dr. Abba on Thursday, the 19th; can you ask Dr. Windsor to go ahead and schedule the procedure for that Friday?" Christine turns into the parking garage and pulls into the first available parking spot.

"You'll need to speak to Dr. Windsor directly to modify the date of your surgical appointment before I can make any changes. Let me see if she is available. One moment, please."

Christine's phone is silent as she is placed on hold; leaving only the muffled roar of the traffic outside the parking garage and the pounding beat of her heart to deafen her ears.

"This is Dr. Windsor." Her familiar voice is a welcome sound, drowning out the ominous noise of the street.

"Hi, Dr. Windsor. It's Christine Becker. I just scheduled an appointment with Dr. Abba, so I wanted to go ahead and get the procedure scheduled."

"I'm sorry, Christine. Procedures of that type usually take a minimum of three weeks to schedule. Don't you think this is a little premature? You may change your mind after the meeting."

"No, I can't say I do. I would like to go ahead and schedule it." Christine's leg starts to shake on the floorboard, as she chews on her thumbnail to relieve the tension growing in her chest.

"If that's what you want to do, Christine. Let's see... I can pencil you in on October 23rd. That's three weeks from Thursday, at 10 a.m."

"Thank you."

"However," Dr. Windsor interjects before Christine can hang up, "I would like to go ahead and bring you in just to check you and the baby out. We didn't get to do that earlier. Could you come in later this week?"

Christine's eyes grow damp at the thought of having to go back into that examination room so soon. "I'm really busy this week. Is there another time?"

"Sure, Christine, how about after your meeting with Dr. Abba? Let's say the 20th, first thing in the morning."

"That's fine," Christine concedes.

She tosses the phone into her purse and exits the car, eager to get to work and away from this nightmare.

———

For Dr. Windsor, days are not really days, but a series of consecutive hours with patients linked together by meals and a few hours of sleep. Unable to commit herself to anyone else, she devotes every waking hour to women, encouraging healthy women and birthing healthy babies into the dreary world created by man. This is her legacy, her contribution to the human race, and she nurtures her baby as any mother would, with diligence and constant vigilance. She enters her office after another full day of patients and consultations. No deliveries today, but tomorrow promises the birth of a new soul. Laying her stethoscope on her desk, she collapses into the waiting arms and comfort of her office chair. Although it is only a little past six, the setting sun creates a cozy glow of yellows, oranges and reds throughout her office, warming Laura's insides like the cup of hot chocolate her mother used to make on cool fall evenings. They would sit wrapped together in a blanket on the sofa, watching *Breakfast at Tiffany's* and *An Affair to Remember* while eating homemade cookies and sipping cocoa. That was back when love was a fairy tale and she was the apple upon which her father doted. Now Laura finds comfort in science, in constant facts. Two plus two will always be four, and what goes up must always come down.

Sitting up straight, Laura Windsor sorts through a few of the day's files collected on her desk. Coming across Christine Becker's chart, she realizes that she has yet to call Dr. Abba to review her file with him. Running her fingers through her hair, she picks up the receiver and dials the number she knows by heart.

"Yes, is Dr. Abba in, please? This is Dr. Windsor."

"Just one moment, please." The robotic voice echoes into the receiver.

Dr. Windsor taps her pencil on the desk as she glances over Christine Becker's file, and waits for Jesse's familiar voice to acknowledge her presence on the other end.

"Laura, so glad you caught me. I was about to call it a day." Jesse's smooth voice immediately comforts her. "It has been a while since we last spoke."

"I know, I know. I've been really busy at work... which is the main reason I am calling, actually. I wanted to talk to you about a patient that I referred, Christine Becker."

"Sure, let's see. Yes, I have her on my schedule for Thursday, the 19th. Tell me what's going on."

"I am really concerned. She just found out she was pregnant today, and wanted to terminate the pregnancy five minutes later. She doesn't even want to consider keeping the baby. Adoption isn't an option, either. She wants it gone, and she wants it to have happened five minutes ago."

"I see. So you're concerned she will regret it?"

Laura knows by his concentrated tone that Jesse is sitting behind his desk, hair disheveled from a long afternoon of sessions, a spare pencil perched behind his right ear as he scratches notes onto a pad. Even in this modern age, Jesse prefers to keep things basic, taking notes the old-fashioned way with legal pad and a number two. But as she pictures his office, she gets it all wrong. Jesse is not sitting in the cozy, dimly lit office that Laura pictures, surrounded by leather-bound books, matching furniture, and a trickling fountain. That was years ago, when they were colleagues. Jesse now sits in a slightly less cozy room with mismatched furniture and sparse shelves — the price you pay for opening a second practice during the same time that insurance scales back your fees, dictates your patient load, and limits your time on each case. The pay-cut has never bothered Jesse, but he refuses to let bureaucracy dictate how he practices. Fighting against the big guys has its price, and it shows in Dr. Abba's lackluster new practice in Mamaroneck. Laura wouldn't know this, of course; she has been too preoccupied for the last three years establishing her own success.

"Well, you understand the human psyche much better than I, but I am concerned that if she goes through with this, she could regret it." Laura leans back in her chair and removes her glasses, revealing tired eyes. No one is there to see them except for the mounds of papers and files and her dog, Max, as he contemplates her through the glass picture frame on her desk.

"Is she married?"

"No."

"Has she ever wanted children?"

"At one time, she expressed an interest in children, which is why I'm concerned. Since she's thirty-eight years old, and might not have another opportunity."

"Is she in a relationship, or is this just an unfortunate circumstance?"

"No relationships; her work is her baby."

"Sounds like someone else I know."

Laura can hear the grin through the miles of phone line that connect them.

"I know. I know. You're not much better yourself."

"Are you sure this isn't counter transference?" he asks again, only half joking.

"You know I never wanted a baby; Max, my 50 pound chocolate lab, is my baby." Tears well up in Laura's eyes, and she struggles to hide the shake in her voice. Somehow Jesse always manages to turn her into a blubbering mess of feelings and tears.

"Laura?"

"Life has been a little tough lately."

"What's going on?"

"It's Max. He's missing, and I can't get anyone to take me seriously." A loud sob escapes her lips. She can't hold it back now. "I tried... to call... the police, but... they are too busy with missing people to worry about... missing dogs."

"Laura, I am so sorry. Is there anything I can do?"

Hearing true concern in Jesse's voice calms Laura slightly, enabling her to regain control over her emotional outburst. "I don't know what to do. I just need him back; he's all I have."

"If I might make a suggestion... I am organizing a support group for people just like you, for people who have had a loved one vanish. Our first meeting will be in a couple of weeks. Would you like to come?"

"I don't know. I've never been one to share with others."

"Well, you must believe it does some good, or you wouldn't refer your patients."

For a quick flash of a second, Laura sees the rest of her lonely life stretched out before her, with no bends or loops in sight. Tired of the heartache and disappointment in life, she has gotten off the ride. Or is it that she is too scared to get back on? Laura yanks her thoughts back to the surface of her mind, unwilling to lose herself to the muck beneath.

Trying to persuade her, Jesse adds, "We could grab a bite to eat afterwards."

"Ok, all right. I'll try it, but no promises." She pauses and then adds, "Thank you, Jesse. You're always pushing me to try new things. I wished we talked more often."

"I do too."

"Well... thanks again, Jesse."

"I'll have my assistant call you with the specifics. It's at my Mamaroneck office."

"Oh, I didn't know you expanded."

"Don't get too excited. I've had to downsize a bit to keep everything afloat."

"Not a problem; I'll look forward to seeing you in a couple of weeks."

"Sounds good. Take care."

Hanging up the receiver, Laura leans over her desk to finish up today's files and prepare for tomorrow's appointments. In a few hours her stomach once again reveals to her the absence of dinner. She rises from her desk, grabs her coat and purse from the coat rack by the door, turns out the light, and closes the door to her office. She picks up chow mein with a side of egg rolls for dinner, even though she has consumed the same meal for the last two days, and she goes home to spend another night in her empty brownstone apartment. Instead of her normal evening stroll through Central Park with Max, she absently consumes her dinner, leaves her clothes on the closet floor when she puts on her nightgown, and falls asleep to the muffled sounds of the television.

⸻

Kevin beats his balled fist against the door.

"Where is she?"

The door groans open to reveal Jesse standing in his bathrobe, hair disheveled from a restless night's sleep. "Where is who?" he questions, rubbing sleep out of the corner of his eye.

"What do you mean 'who'? Where the hell is my wife?"

Shoving Jesse out of his way, Kevin marches into the apartment. His eyes dart around the sparse living room on his way down the hall to the bedroom.

"Oh. She's not here," Jesse yells after him, bending down to pick up the morning's newspaper from the hallway.

"I know she *was* here. I heard her yesterday ... through the wall. Do you think I am stupid? That I don't know what's going on?"

Looking for clues of Kate's presence, Kevin makes his way back through the living room into the adjoining kitchen, where Jesse leans against the counter fixing his morning cup of coffee as if he hasn't heard him at all.

"You're sleeping together. Aren't you?" Kevin holds his clinched fists down at his side, willing himself not to break him. After his stint in Iraq, he knows several ways to accomplish this. Another nasty side effect that no one talks about, fighting with fists and guns instead of coffee and words. The anger and the guilt never go away, even after the bombs and guns vanish, and heroes return to the tiny little spaces they once occupied. But they aren't the same shape they used to be. A little harder around the edges, a little bent from the weight of war, just enough that they don't fit so neatly, so perfectly into their past life. Jaded and hung over, Kevin awaits confirmation from the accused.

Jesse turns to face him.

"No, we are not. Look. I barely know your wife. We met at a tenant's meeting a couple of weeks ago and became friends. Just friends. She was here yesterday asking for sugar, we talked a little bit, and then she left for work. That's all." His smooth, calm voice echoes through the sparse kitchen and reverberates within each individual cell of Kevin's brain as they absorb and grasp the meaning of Jesse's words.

With coffee in hand and newspaper tucked under his arm, Jesse passes Kevin as he walks into the living room. Kevin follows behind.

"I don't understand... I heard her in here yesterday morning, and now she is gone. No note, nothing. Where is she?" Talking more to himself than to Jesse, Kevin doesn't expect an answer.

Jesse lowers himself into a frayed green armchair, careful not to spill the hot coffee on his lower extremities. He smells the stagnant stench of alcohol as Kevin begins to pace. He's heard the yelling and the shatter of glass through the same thin walls that merely muffled the despairing cadence of Kate's voice, the voice Kevin has so often ignored. Jesse combs his fingers through his hair, a failed attempt to wrangle it in.

"Why don't you have a seat? It's Kevin, right?"

Kevin nods as he plops onto the worn leather couch, resigning himself to the possibility that Kate has left him.

"I'll fix you some coffee. You look like you could use it just as much as I could. I think we have both had some late nights recently."

"I guess you've heard us, uh?" Kevin drops his head into his hands, his elbow digging into his knees. "I just don't understand why she won't talk to me anymore. She'll apparently talk to complete strangers, but not her own *husband*. All we do is scream and break things. She's probably said more to you in a single morning than she's said to me in the past three months."

Jesse comes back with a second cup of coffee. Kevin mumbles thanks.

"Well, why do you think that is?" Jesse questions softly as he returns to the green hand-me-down armchair across from him.

"I think she's tired of putting up with me. Can't say that I blame her. I can't stand me much, either."

"Actually," Jesse interrupts, "I can tell that she loves you very much."

"She loves who I used to be."

"Maybe so. But you should know the only reason she talks with me is because she found out that I'm a therapist at the last tenant meeting."

"You're a shrink?"

Jesse smiles. "Yes."

"I'm out of here." Kevin rises to leave.

"Do you watch the news, Kevin?" Jesse interjects, sliding to the end of the cushion in an attempt to hold Kevin there.

"No, I haven't lately. I've been a little preoccupied." Kevin stops. His face flushes slightly to reveal his embarrassment. "Besides, it's only bad news. I've got enough of that already." He steps again toward the door.

"Do you think Kate may be missing like the others?"

Kevin turns to face him squarely. "What others?"

"People have been disappearing in record numbers. I think the total rose to 15,000 this morning. You should check with her co-workers before jumping to any conclusions. Kate loves you, Kevin. I've seen it. She wouldn't just give up, no matter how bad things are." Jesse sips his coffee, letting it warm his mouth before swallowing hard.

"I didn't know about the others." Kevin walks over to Jesse. "Thanks." He hands Jesse his half-empty mug and then heads for the door.

"Oh, and, uh ... sorry for barging in." Kevin disappears behind the door in one quick motion.

Still sitting in his threadbare armchair, Jesse opens the newspaper and takes another sip of his morning coffee. Skimming through, he absorbs all of the important headlines, bold across the page, and then carefully studies the morning's political cartoon. Reaching the end, he leaves the comfort of his broken-in armchair for the equal pleasure of a warm shower. Dressing in his signature style of jeans, untucked button-up shirt, and cardigan, he heads out to greet the beautiful fall weather and his first client of the day.

———

While time is nothing but the succession of seconds, minutes, and hours strung together with an invisible string, linking one event to another, it seems to Christine like an uninvited house guest that will never leave. For two weeks, time has tormented her, laughing at her with the constant tick-tick-tick of the hands moving slowly around the clock. Unable to concentrate on her fraud investigation or the president's missing child, she focuses only on the seconds ticking away into minutes, minutes into hours, until her appointment with Dr. Abba.

The day finally arrives, and Christine's clock alerts her to the fact that it is time for her morning run. Awake and anticipating the sound, she silences the beeps with a swift swat of her hand and rises from the bed. Combing her fingers through her hair, she gathers her long chestnut -colored tresses into a pony tail. Holding the gathered bunch with one hand, she removes the hair-tie from her wrist with her teeth and pulls her hair through it several times, yanking it tight. She throws on a pair of jogging pants and a long-sleeved tee and slips her feet into the running shoes waiting beside her bed. She has three and a half more hours to wait — two hundred and ten minutes, twelve thousand, six-hundred seconds. But who's counting?

Christine grabs her house key and slips it down into her sports bra for safekeeping, then heads out the door and down the steps to confront the cold waiting for her outside. It appears that she is the only one awake on the West Side as she stretches her legs at the bottom of the steps. Even the sun remains under its nighttime covers, the street lamps lighting her way as she begins to run down the usual streets. The crisp autumn air fills her lungs, reminding her of when she was four years old, her daddy pushing her on the swing. She loved the sensation of soaring up in to the sky and then falling weightlessly down, only for her father to send her flying again. But now, she runs. A futile attempt to regain something from the past she lost or an equally futile attempt to flee that awful something she can't shake, that something seemingly minuscule in purpose but growing to consume her. Whatever the reason, Christine runs with the dedication of a Catholic going to daily mass, allowing her body to ache with exertion and freeing her mind to think of nothing.

Arriving back at her building sweaty and tired, she lumbers up the three flights of stairs to her flat, removes the key from her undergarment, and slips into her apartment. She undresses as she makes her way through the living room and into her bedroom to take a shower. She takes her time washing the film of salt and sweat that has gathered on her skin, attempting to calm her nerves and focus on something other than the small human developing within her womb. She washes and rinses her hair gently, running conditioner through the full length of it while feeling the water cascade on top of her head. She stands still for a brief moment, allowing the water to pour over her before turning it off and grabbing a towel hanging nearby. She checks the time and dresses for the day. At eight o'clock, Christine calls into *The Times* to let Hal know she will be in late. Migraine. She hangs up the phone, grabs her coat, and hails a cab on the corner. Arriving early, as is her custom, Christine enters Dr. Abba's office and signs in with his administrative assistant. Sitting and attempting to wait patiently, thumbing through magazines yet again, never has Christine spent so much time glancing through glamorized gossipy garbage.

"Dr. Abba is ready to see you." His assistant opens the door. Christine throws the magazine on the end table and follows her down the hallway. Christine is now able to put a face to the robotic voice that spoke to her from the other end of the phone.

"Hi, Dr. Abba. Nice to meet you." Christine extends her hand to shake his, even though they both know this is the last place she wants to be.

"It's nice to meet you, too, Christine. Please call me Jesse. Everyone else does." Jesse smiles. "Take a seat... anywhere you would like." There are only a few chairs in the office from which to choose, so Christine sits in the closest one to her and the door, a chair-and-a-half that a small child could get lost in. Christine balances on the edge of the cushion, hopeful that this won't take long.

"Dr. Windsor gave me a brief overview of your situation, but I would like to hear it from you. So, what brings you here today, Christine?"

"Well, I guess it is fairly straightforward. I made a mistake two months ago, and now I am pregnant. I don't want to be, but Dr. Windsor won't do the procedure without your clearance. I just need you to tell her I am of sound mind and that we can proceed with this and stop dragging out the inevitable."

"That's pretty much what she told me... not quite in those terms, but to the same point." Jesse sits down in the chair opposite her and crosses one leg over the other to balance his notepad. "She mentioned that you spoke of wanting a child, but now you are adamant about not being a mom. What do you think changed?"

Still perched on the edge of the chair, Christine releases a small sigh of contrition. "Things change. Priorities change. I didn't plan on getting pregnant. It just happened."

"How did it happen?"

"Really?"

"Do you want my signature? Yes? So, enlighten me."

"Fine, have it your way." Christine can see that there is no escape, so she leans back to settle in for the prequel that got her here in the first place. "Johnny, my best friend of 30 years, and I were celebrating because I had just received this big award. We started drinking, one toast leading to the next. That, by the way, is totally uncharacteristic of me; so, as you can imagine, I ended up a little wasted. Being the gentleman that he is, Johnny walked me to my hotel room... next thing I remember we were kissing in the middle of the hall way. It was really weird at first, you know. I have known this guy my whole life and never thought of him in that way. But then we kissed again... and the next thing I know, it's 4:30 in the morning, I've got a massive hangover, and Johnny is lying next to me. At first I was confused... when I saw him lying there – naked – but then everything from the night before flashed through my mind. I felt so humiliated that I slipped out of the bed, went for a run, and lingered even more by stopping for breakfast, hoping he would be gone when I got back. When I returned, he was in the shower. Singing! I still couldn't face him, so I left him a note apologizing, telling him how important he was to me and that I hope I didn't screw things up. Then I went back to my apartment."

"So how does he feel about the baby?"

"He doesn't know." Feeling vulnerable in the space, Christine draws her knee up to her chest and hugs her arms tightly around her thin leg.

"Don't you think you should discuss it with him?"

"No, it's my career."

"How does your career change the fact that you are carrying his baby?"

Frustrated by the questioning, she changes the subject. "Have you ever seen a pregnant journalist win a Pulitzer?"

"So it doesn't happen this year. You won't have more chances in the future? I think you are a little young for retirement."

" I hate being pregnant. Losing control of my body stresses me out."

"If I may... it seems to me you are acting out of fear and that you are not weighing the pros and cons of what you are really doing. Considering you confided in Dr. Windsor that you really wanted a child less than a year ago, I would like you to just take a little time and search for what your heart truly desires. The decision you make will stay with you for the rest of your life."

Jesse pauses for a brief moment to let that settle on the rough edges of Christine's brain. "Plus, it sounds like you really care for your friend, and a secret like this can be life-altering to a relationship."

Christine still doesn't respond.

"I would like to see you again next week." Jesse unfolds himself from his chair, waiting for Christine to do the same, but she remains seated, staring at him in disbelief, mouth slightly ajar, forehead crinkled.

"Dr. Abba, I have the procedure already scheduled for next Thursday. I need you to sign off on the paperwork and let me deal with my own guilt-riddled future!"

"Unfortunately, Christine, that is not an option. You will just have to trust my professional judgment. I will see you next Wednesday. If you have done what I asked, you can still have the procedure on Thursday."

"This is ridiculous!" Christine shouts.

"My secretary will schedule you on the way out. Try to have a good day, Christine. Stress isn't good for the baby."

"You know this is a complete waste of my time, don't you?" Christine jumps up and snatches her bag off the seat.

"Only time will tell. I'll see you on Wednesday?" Jesse smiles in an attempt to ease the tension that is rapidly filling the room.

"Do I have a choice?" Christine turns and walks to the door, slamming it shut behind her.

For the last few weeks, work has been a struggle for Christine. The inability to focus is showing in her sloppy exposé on the investment fraud article and her lack of effort to research the disappearances. It's not from a lack of trying. Christine sits at her desk, willing her brain to function, trying to focus on the task in front of her, but her harried thoughts drift inevitably to the soul growing in her belly. Today, she works later than normal. "Put in a full day," she says to herself, "to make up for my absence this morning." The truth is that she is not quite ready to go home, to be alone with the thoughts gnawing away at her spirit. However, no one – not even Christine – knows that's the reason she stays.

Her body continues to occupy her desk, to stare at the computer screen and the blinking cursor that remains at the top left corner of the page. Her mind is elsewhere, festering over the unfair cards that have been dealt so casually in her direction. Finally deciding that enough is enough for one day, Christine shuts down the blank computer screen, grabs the coat off the back of her chair, and heads for the elevator.

She can't remember much about the train ride home or the block-and-a-half walk to her apartment building. Operating on autopilot, Christine finds herself exhausted and frustrated as she enters her barely lived-in living room. She falls onto her sofa, letting herself sink into the oversized cushions. Propping her feet on the coffee table, she reaches for the remote resting on the end table. With thoughts of Dr. Abba and his frustrating unwillingness to sign whirling around in her brain, she flicks through the channels, settling on CNN. She listens to the weatherman's forecast that it will be a beautiful day, as he stands in front of the all-so-familiar green screen. She hears her stomach growl for the fifth time and attempts to motivate herself to get off the couch for something to eat. She unfolds herself from the clutches of the sofa and moseys into the kitchen to heat up a frozen dinner.

The television grabs her attention as the news anchor shifts to national news. She stands in the doorway, watching the TV and listening for the microwave to beep.

"Breaking news. We have just been alerted that the number of disappearances is now totaling 22,000 people in the US, and the hunt continues for the men responsible for kidnapping the president's daughter, Grace." The news anchor's voice adapts the appropriate tone of solemnity as she continues reporting. The microwave beeps, signaling to Christine that her meal waits. She steps over to grab the plastic tray by the tips of her fingers and hurries into the living room, setting it down on the coffee table. She waits, anticipating the next report.

"In response to the current crisis, riots have broken out in the streets, and crime is reaching an all-time high Robert Hunt, a 27-year-old Caucasian male residing in Brooklyn, almost beat an Iranian cab driver to death before police arrived to arrest him. As there appears to be no clear motive, police are investigating this as a hate crime. It is rumored that Robert's wife disappeared two weeks ago. Hunt is currently being held without bail. His arraignment is scheduled for next Tuesday."

Christine slouches back into the couch and holds the plastic tray of food under her mouth as she watches the news reporter shift in her chair. She blows onto the steaming forkful of food and places it gingerly into her mouth.

"In national news, there is growing concern surrounding the stability of the First Lady. In seclusion for the third straight week since the disappearance of her only daughter Grace, the First Lady is rumored to be suffering from severe depression. Our thoughts and prayers go out to her and others struggling with the disappearance of a loved one."

Unable to take anymore of the depressing news, Christine places the empty tray on the coffee table and turns off the television. She then goes into the kitchen, disposes of the microwaved tray, wipes the counters, checks the front door, turns off the lights and heads into her bedroom.

"Honey, I'm heading out to see Lexi. I should be home around four." Anna Marie straightens up a few loose pieces of mail at the end of the counter and digs in her purse for her keys.

"What? You're leaving? You do realize our son Brian is missing, don't you?" Anna Marie's husband, Zack, rises from the breakfast table and slips across the kitchen floor in his socks to put the dirty dishes in the sink. He reaches over in an effort to grab the dirty sippy cup that has been sitting on the edge of the counter for months. "Don't you think it's important that we focus on finding him? He probably ran away because you don't...."

"What are you doing?" Anna Marie shouts. "Put that sippy cup back! Put it BACK! That's Lexi's. She'll want that when she comes home..." Silence fills the air. "And I do care about Brian. I do. He has you looking after him. I know you'll find him. I just have to go. I have to be with her... You don't understand. You'll never understand."

"She's my daughter, too, you know. I don't think you understand *that!*"

"I know that, Zack!"

"I can't do this anymore, Annie. I need my wife back. I'm grieving, too," he declares. There's a long pause as Anna Marie says nothing. "You need to get some help, or I'm leaving."

Anna Marie stares at Zack, disbelief on her face. In the twenty years of their marriage, they have never spoken such words in anger.

Anna Marie and Zack met twenty years ago as freshmen at South Brooklyn Community High School. They were in the same English class but sat at opposite ends of the room. Both noticed each other but were unwilling to be the first to speak. The semester went on without a proper introduction, but then the teacher assigned a presentation: each group was to cover a story from Chaucer's *Canterbury Tales*. As if by fate, the teacher assigned Anna Marie and Zack to work together. Not being strong in English, Zach convinced her to do the bulk of the project in return for tutoring her in advanced AP Physics and dinner anywhere she wanted. After each received an "A" on the project, Anne Marie chose the most expensive deli in town.

They surprised everyone by getting married right out of high school. Anna Marie was very attractive, with wits to match and her parents had hoped she would go to college before settling down. Zack, a techie interested more in computers and gaming than sitting in a classroom talking about sonnets and hydrogen bombs, chose the entrepreneurial route instead of college.

Anna Marie's family secretly hoped she would meet someone else; but people can't choose who they love, they can only choose whether or not to make it work. Anna Marie and Zack chose to make it work. Living paycheck to paycheck in a rented basement apartment that leaked when it rained and smelled dank and musty when it didn't, they believed they were living a charmed life, even though it was located in a less than desirable area of Brooklyn. Zack eventually started a small tech company out of a damp corner in their basement apartment, a company that went public seven years after they married and netted $5.2 million dollars before he turned twenty-five. They moved to the other side of the Brooklyn Bridge into the Big Apple Landing in Battery Park City. Two years and a stock-market windfall later, they moved to Mamaroneck, New York, and celebrated with the birth of their first-born, Brian. The possession of money didn't changed who they were, generous people, who donated thousands yearly to this charity or that. The only extravagance they allowed themselves was a membership to the prestigious Hampershire County Club, a decision that would permanently alter their lives. A few years passed, bringing them the birth of another child, this time a daughter named Lexi. For Zack, Lexi captured the stars in her eyes and holds the universe in her hand. Lexi was a daddy's girl.

Unable to look at his wife's pleading face, he storms past her and up the stairs to the bedroom. Anna Marie plops helplessly onto a barstool and stares at the photographs on the wall, happy memories of camp-outs at the lake and holiday vacations at the shore. A few seconds later, she hears the heavy footsteps of her husband as he races down the stairs and out of the house, slamming the door behind him. The walls shake behind the force of his hand, and a picture tumbles off the small nail protruding from the wall. The shattering of glass awakens Anna Marie from her thoughts, as she gasps "No!" and races to pick up the remnants of the broken frame. Staring back at her through splintered shards of glass are four happy faces sitting in front of the Christmas tree. The picture was taken over a year ago, back when the smiles weren't forced and her family was happy and intact. Anna Marie gently runs her finger over the smiling face of her daughter.

"He doesn't understand. He never will. It wasn't his fault."

A fog creeps down and into her brain, blocking all other thoughts. She wipes a tear from her cheek and places the broken frame on the counter. She grabs her purse and leaves the mess for later. Digging once again in her purse for the keys, she finds the power bill she forgot to mail last week. She walks to the mailbox to place it inside. As she pulls the flag up, she notices a flyer attached, an invitation to join a therapy group for people affected by the recent epidemic of disappearances. She glances over it and shoves it in her purse for later. Right now, her five year old daughter is waiting for her to brush her hair and to learn the ending of *Anne of Green Gables*.

As promised, Christine sits in the waiting room, shaking her leg and waiting for the attendant to call her name. Dr. Windsor usually runs a tight ship with on-schedule appointments, but today, Christine has been waiting for twenty minutes. Twenty minutes too long, for now she has time to think.

She has been keeping busy, or at least attempting to keep busy. She continues her morning run, adding on an extra mile to compensate for her unusual craving for peanut butter and hamburgers with all of the fixings. She has been treading water at work, unable to catch a lead and only able to maintain a focus that is foggy at best. Dr. Windsor would probably say she is in denial, and she would probably be right; but Christine will never admit it. In the twenty minutes waiting with nothing to do but think, she starts to wonder. The idea forms in her mind like an itch in the back of the throat that can't be scratched: the realization that a human life is growing in her belly and unexpectedly, the heartbeat of its unborn body will reach her ears momentarily.

The attendant calls Christine's name twice to break her from her trance.

"Ms. Becker? ... Ms. Becker? Dr. Windsor's assistant will see you now."

"Oh...," Christine mutters as she rises to follow her to the examination room.

Christine enters the familiar room on the left with the pictures of happy women with babies in the womb. She places her things in the chair beside the examination table and climbs up to sit and wait. Mercifully, the nurse practitioner is prompt, knocking on the door and entering with a chipper greeting.

"Good morning, Christine. How are you feeling today?" Scanning over her chart, the nurse continues, "Any more morning sickness?"

"Look, can we skip the chit-chat? I need to get to work." Christine looks down at her toes and makes a quick mental note to schedule a pedicure, anything to keep her mind off the task at hand.

The nurse's wrinkled forehead betrays her irritation at Christine's flippant disregard for human life, but Christine doesn't acknowledge the gesture, for she is lost in her own personal hell filled with anxiety, fear, and regret.

"Very well, please lie back on the table." The nurse busies herself with the necessary gels and mechanisms needed to detect the faint thump-thump of a baby's heart. "I'll need you to pull your shirt up a bit."

Christine lies flat on the table and awkwardly slides her shirt up to reveal her slender stomach. The nurse places the cold gel onto the revealed skin and attempts to locate the tiny peanut in the vast womb. Christine tries to ignore the sounds coming from deep inside her belly. Then she hears it, soft at first, and then louder. Thump-thump, thump-thump. A smile creeps over Christine's face. Such a beautiful sound… like the sound she heard laying against Johnny's chest, so welcoming, so safe. Tears form in the corner of her eyes. She manages to wipe them away with her finger, all except one that trickles down her temple and puddles in her ear.

"I can't do this!" Christine rolls off the side of the table, grabs her purse, and bolts through the door of the examining room, leaving the nurse holding the useless ultrasound wand in her hand and a dumbfounded expression on her face. Christine sprints down the hall, into the lobby, and out through the main door.

The cool autumn air greets her and burns her wet cheeks. Through blurry vision, she makes it to the street corner to hail a cab. She climbs into the back seat and drops her head into her hands. "Where to?" the cabby asks, ignoring Christine's obvious emotional state. Her body heaves in unison with her sobs. For the second time today, Christine allows the fear and uncertainty to consume her. She wants to confide in Johnny, to ask him what she should do. She has played the scenario a thousand times over this morning alone. What would he say? What would he want her to do? It is this thought that always stops her. She doesn't want to know what he would want her to do! It should be her choice, not his. Johnny has always been the person Christine went to in times of uncertainty. He always knows the right thing to say, always knows how to comfort her. Deep down inside, she knows he would want her to keep it. So she hangs up the already dialed phone for the third time today.

"Lady, can you help me out here?" The cabby's voice brings her back to reality. She leans forward and clears her throat. She holds her breath to control the heaving of her body, and digs in her purse for a tissue. "I don't know where to go," and then, she loses it again. The cab driver grunts and then pleads with her, "Lady, I'm trying to make a living here." Christine attempts to catch her breath and dries her eyes again. "Ok, ok," she barks back. Flipping down the compact in her purse, she sees the smear of mascara underneath her eyes.

"I can't go to work like this," Christine mutters. Running through the Rolodex of options in her mind, she flips to the most logical choice: Dr. Abba. Determination slowly migrates across her faces as she professes, "I'm putting an end to this today." She announces, "Fifty-ninth and Lex-" Before she can finish her command, she is thrown backwards in the seat as the driver speeds away.

The door to Dr. Abba's waiting room swings open with a loud screech and reveals Christine's rumpled silhouette. Her mascara has been wiped clean, but her cheeks are splotchy and her eyes swollen and red. Closing the door, she approaches the secretary who looks up at her with a pleasant smile. Something about her smile irritates Christine, sweetness so sickeningly artificial that chewing tinfoil would be more enjoyable.

"I need to see Dr. Abba immediately. This can't wait until Thursday." The words slip and slide past her clinched teeth.

"I am sorry, Ms. Becker. Dr. Abba is in session right now, but he has a short break between clients in about 45 minutes. Would you like to wait?" Her slippery smile reemerges, clashing with her metallic voice and raising the bile in Christine's stomach.

"I guess I have no other choice. So, yes I'll wait." Christine forces a thin smile and joins the dated furniture and magazines in the waiting room.

Hommocks Middle School isn't much different from other middle schools. It stretches and sprawls between the arms of Hommocks Park and Hampshire Country Club. The halls smell of paper, ink, and spoiled milk; and are filled with a mixture of rich kids from the Club and poor kids from the west side of town. A typical school, in a typical town, where everything is routine. In the principal's office, Diane Couch slouches over the folds of skin and polyester as she waits for the final verdict.

If Diane were a science experiment, she would be the control group, ever constant, predictable. For the past fifteen years, Diane has taught eighth grade science, preaching on and on in front of the class about osmosis, tectonic plates, and the periodic table. Even her marriage cannot escape the confines of complacency. Buy groceries on Sunday, serve meatloaf on Wednesdays, have sex on Fridays, and watch *Wheel of Fortune* at 7:30 every day of the week. Today is Thursday, so she will go home to pot roast, a recliner, and *X Factor*. Everything in its proper time and place. But last week, her regimen was broken. Diane's husband, Ben, did not come home from the power plant.

Principal Skinner leans forward, resting his arms on the top of his desk and intertwining his fingers. His voice is soft, with a hint of reassurance. "Diane, this can't continue. I have had three complaints in the last week."

Diane shakes her head in absent comprehension, a blank expression on her face. Since her husband left, she comes to work but sits at her desk and stares into space, occasionally interjecting an assignment or an ineffective warning to quiet down. The remnants of a spitball glisten as the sun passes through the thin strands of her graying hair. Yesterday, Principal Skinner noticed her standing at the front of the class, writing science terms on the blackboard with a "kick me" sign taped to her back, oblivious to the rambunctious adolescents texting and talking behind her.

He leans back in his chair and folds his arms across his chest. His glasses have slipped down his nose, stopped by the regal bump protruding in the middle of it. "Now, I know that things have been difficult for you lately. I am willing to work with you on this, but you have to meet me halfway." He reaches over to the top right drawer of his heavy, oversized desk, pulls it out a few inches, and takes out a card. He then slides it across the smooth glossy surface toward Diane. "You might find it helpful to talk with someone. I have referred people to this guy in the past. He's really good and might just be able to help you through this."

Diane reaches for the card, glances at the conservative print, and tucks it in the pocket of her baggy trousers. "Yes, sir." Her mind drifts to the pot roast in the crock pot, wondering if she remembered to turn it down before she left that morning.

"You've got some days built up. Why don't you take the rest of the week off, call Dr. Abba, and come back in refreshed? I will arrange a sub. It will do you some good."

The drive home is uneventful. Diane notices Mr. Booker mowing his lawn instead of waiting for Saturday morning to roll around. Ben always mows the grass on Saturday morning, and for a moment, Diane can almost hear the dueling push-mowers, each one racing to finish its patch of grass first. But it's not Saturday, and Ben is gone.

As she pulls into her drive, she is confronted with his absence. The grass is taller than it has even been under the diligence of her husband, and within a week, weeds have crept into her meticulous flower beds. The car no longer running, Diane stares at, but doesn't really see, the slats in the garage door. The garage has been cleaned out for months now (cleaning had become Ben's way of coping).

Normally, she would enter the house, kiss Ben hello (he would be on day shift this week), and start pulling the dishes from the cabinets and the roast from the crock pot; but everything is off. She is home early, Ben isn't home, and the pot roast still needs a couple of hours on low. Unsure of what to do with her unexpected free time, Diane pushes herself from the driver's side of her two-door hatchback, and walks the short but still exhausting distance to the front door and the loneliness that waits to greet her.

The front door lock has always been difficult to open, but over the years she has come to master the trick of pressing with her knee while twisting the key. She doesn't even notice anymore, even though Ben has offered to replace it many times. She greets the loneliness with a sigh and goes through the living room, past Ben's empty recliner, and into the kitchen. She lifts the lid to the crock pot and breathes in the comforting aroma. Just a few more hours, and the roast will be right on time. Diane sits at the kitchen table and stares at the pile of mail collected there. She slides her hands down her thighs and hears the crinkle of the business card in her pocket. She lays it on the table in front of her and on top of the overdue notices and credit card applications. Staring once again at the tiny compact print on the card, Diane reaches for the phone.

The phone rings, and a robotic voice answers. For a brief moment, Diane thinks it is an automated service, the "press-1-for" type. She almost loses her nerve, and then the voice repeats, "Dr. Abba's office. Can I help you?"

"Yes, I'm sorry. My name is Diane, and I would like to make an appointment."

"Have you seen Dr. Abba before?"

The tight waiting room makes it difficult for Christine to ignore the receptionist's conversation. The design of the office is definitely not HIPAA-compliant.

"Would you like an individual appointment? Or would you like to participate in the group therapy starting a week from Monday?"

There is a pause, and the waiting room once again grows silent. Christine can only guess at the response on the other end of the line.

"It's a special group therapy session that Dr. Abba is starting, in response to the rash of disappearances."

There is another pause as the receptionist listens to the invisible client on the other end. At the mention of disappearances, Christine's ears perk up. Unable to hear as much as she likes, she moves to a closer seat under the pretense of retrieving a different magazine.

"The sessions are on Monday night at eight. He anticipates the sessions will last about two hours, but will go longer if necessary."

Again a pause, and a superfluous smile reaches the receptionist's lips.

"In two weeks... Will that work?" The quick fingers of the receptionist echo through the small space. "I've got you down, Ms. Couch. See you then."

The office is once again silent except for the whirling sound of the gears turning in Christine's brain.

"Excuse me. Is there a restroom I can use? I can't hold it like I used to," she smiles.

The receptionist points to a door on the opposite wall without any acknowledgement of Christine's attempt at humor. Undeterred, Christine heads to the designated door, closes it behind her, and locates her phone from within the depths of her bag.

Finding Joanne's number on speed dial, she taps her foot impatiently on the floor.

"*New York Times*. Joanne..."

"Joanne, it's me."

"Christine? I can hardly hear you. Where are you? Why are you whispering?"

"I've got it. You are not going to believe this..." Christine pauses for effect.

"Well, I'm waiting..."

"Okay. There is a group therapy session starting in a couple of weeks, centered on all of these missing people. I'm going to join it."

"Christine, haven't you heard of ethics? You can't put any of that in print. Besides, you haven't had anyone you know disappear. The closest connection you have is the server at the coffee shop."

"I'm not going to divulge anything discussed in the sessions, but it could help me find a link, you know, a common thread. And you're wrong — I have had someone I love disappear. At least as far as the group will know."

"Okay. I admit it might have potential. Hey, look. I've got to go. Hal's been breathing down my neck. But I'd like to know why is it *you* always manage to be in the right place at the right time?" Christine places the phone back in her bag and flushes the toilet for effect. She emerges from the bathroom and returns to her chair and magazine in the waiting room.

The slippery sound of pages turning bounces softly across the room. Christine turns them in a rhythmic succession of movements, calm and focused on the tasks at hand: Dr. Abba's consent for the surgery and getting into that group.

"Dr. Abba will see you now." The receptionist chirps in her direction as a shaggy man in cargo pants and v-neck clomps to the door and exits the office. Christine tosses the magazine back on the table and enters the sparse office where Dr. Abba waits for her, dwarfed by the mountain of paperwork stacked on the oversized desk.

"Christine, this is unexpected. What can I do for you today?" Dr Abba greets her with a smile.

"I have the answer to your question, so I would appreciate your signing off on my case."

"Oh... Well, that's good. What does your heart want, Christine?"

"It wants to not feel sad."

"Good. And how did you stumble onto this truth?"

"I left Dr. Windsor' s office and couldn't stop crying. So there's your answer."

"Okay. And what was it that made you cry?"

"Why does that matter?"

"Humor me."

"I heard the baby's heart beat."

"And that made you sad?"

"No."

"So were they tears of joy or of sadness?"

"Well, first it was tears of joy, which was then flooded by sadness. So now I know what I want," Christine determines.

"Really?"

"Yes, really."

"I'm not convinced. You must search your heart to find out why you are blocking your feelings of joy. When you can answer that question, I will release you from my care," Dr. Abba decides.

"Really, are you serious?" She catches herself. "Can I come to your group?"

"I'm sorry?"

"If I do this, can I come to your group two weeks from Monday?"

"No, I'm sorry, Christine. It's a closed group only for those who have lost someone."

"But I have lost someone!"

"Strange. You never mentioned it. Who is missing in your life?"

"My mother."

"Very well." A flicker of disbelief shines briefly in his eyes, "You can join us."

Christine slides to the front of the chair and hoists herself up with her arms. "Thanks, Dr. Abba. I appreciate it. Oh, and I'll still be back for my appointment this Wednesday, so you can sign off on me. I will get the procedure done on Thursday."

"I am sure you will, Christine." He smiles at her.

She pauses at the door long enough to return the smile and then quietly slips out.

"I am sure you will," Dr. Abba repeats to himself as he straightens the disorganized piles of paper on his desk.

Anna Marie closes the door behind her. She has just finished reading the last chapter of *Anne of Green Gables*, and it's time to go home and cook dinner. Leaving Lexi is always the hardest part of her day; kissing her goodbye and leaving her in a cold hospital room alone is almost unbearable. She has tried to make the room as cozy as possible by hanging butterfly posters and bringing her ladybug comforter from home, but how can she leave her baby alone to find her way back in the dark? She always leaves a lamp on so if Lexi wakes up while she's gone, she won't be afraid. For six months, Anna Marie spent every second by her side, crying in between the "I'm-so-sorries," and "I-love-yous." Finally, Zack made Anna Marie come home at night, but she still doesn't sleep. She cries into her pillow and waits for the sun to bring another day and another chance for a miracle.

Anna Marie clicks down the hospital corridor in her sandals, operating on autopilot. Spending a year in the maze of halls, she could walk this route blindfolded. She reaches into her purse for her phone. Unable to locate it, she plunks the purse down on the counter of the nurses' station and begins to scatter items onto the clean surface. The phone emerges from the bottom of her bag, and Anna Marie begins to place the contents back inside.

"Can I help you?" The on-duty nurse walks over to the counter, a cup of coffee clenched in her hand.

"Oh..." She looks at the mess of papers on the counter. "No, thanks... I'm just looking for something." She attempts a smile but is not successful as she gives her cell phone a wave, as if to indicate she doesn't make a habit of leaving messes.

A folded piece of paper slides off of the counter and flutters down to rest on the floor. She shoves the remaining items on the counter back into her purse and bends down to retrieve the flyer. Unable to remember what it is, she unfolds it carefully, holding the corners with the tips of her fingers. Dr. Abba's name, printed in bold block font, stares back at her. Glancing over it, she remembers it from earlier that morning, folded between the red flag and mailbox. As she stares at it, her thoughts drift to Zack and, for the first time, to Brian. Perhaps this would show Zack she is trying, that she is getting help the way he asked her to. Her gut clenches at the thought of baring her soul and her mistakes in front of strangers, but she has no other choice. She needs more time, and this is the perfect way to get it. Her steps quicken as she approaches the hospital door. Once outside she dials the numbers printed on the flyer.

"Yes, my name is Anna Marie, and I want to join that therapy session."

"The number of mysterious disappearances has now risen to an unimaginable 28,000 nationwide, and there is still no break in the kidnapping of nine-year-old Grace. The First Lady, however, has ended her seclusion and is now arranging an International Day of Prayer." The television screen flips from the perfectly coiffed news anchor to a snippet of the First Lady speaking at a press conference earlier that day. She looks tired and aged somehow, as if years have passed in the matter of weeks. No one knows the strength of a mother's love nor the pull of the tether that binds her to her child. "It is my hope that we can come together as a nation, and as a world, to stop this, to find our missing loved ones, and to unify religions of the world, even if it is just for a few hours one day of the year. My hope is that this becomes a beginning of peace." The television returns to the poised news anchor. "In local news…"

Christine and Joanne pause to listen to the lengthy list of violent hate crimes that have occurred since the initial disappearances. It's apparent that there is an underlying fear and anxiety throughout the country, questioning who will be next. Lost in the brutality and horror, neither one notices the waiter standing next to their table.

"Uhhh... Can I get you something to eat or drink?" The waiter barely looks thirteen, with severe acne and shaggy hair. His slim body reminds Christine of Johnny's fit physique in high school, but she quickly discards the thought.

"Sure. I'm starving. I'll have a hamburger with potato salad instead of fries, a green salad, and can I get a side of black-bean-corn salsa?" Christine turns her face from the menu to the young waiter. Joanne's mouth gaps in disbelief.

"Sure."

"Great. Oh, and I'll have an iced tea with that. Do you want anything, Joanne?"

"Umm... yeah." Still trying to wrap her mind around the odd behavior of her dearest friend, Joanne fumbles her words. "I, uh... I'll have the, uh, hamburger, too, but with fries and a Coke."

"Sure thing." The waiter scribbles on his notepad. "I'll get this order in." He strolls off in the direction of the kitchen.

Alone once more at the small table in the back corner, Joanna leans in close, elbows folded on the table. "Are you sure you're not pregnant?" Joanne whispers without a hint of sarcasm.

"What are you talking about?"

"First of all, it's not like it's a crime, and second, in the 10 years I've known you, I have never seen you eat a burger — much less more than 400 calories at any one meal. No wonder you're puking." Then a smile spreads across Joanne's lips and turns into a quick fit of laughter. "Wait... who am I talking to? 'Miss I-don't-even-date'... If you are pregnant, it would have to be the Immaculate Conception."

"Aren't you funny! Actually, I have a serious question to ask you."

"Shoot."

"Do you think I have joy in my life?" Christine asked.

"Do you want a serious answer?"

"Yes."

"If you have to ask someone if you have joy in your life, chances are you don't."

"How do you know?"

"Because I have joy in my life. I have joy every day when my three-year-old hugs me and then demands that my husband hug me at the same time so we can have a triangle kiss; or when I tuck my little one in at night, listening to his prayers; or when I've had a couple of long nights and my husband brings me breakfast in bed and rubs my feet and a couple of other places." Joanna raises her eyebrows up and down, hubba-hubba style.

Christine looks away as the fluorescent lights glitter off the puddles of water forming in her eyes. Joanna observes her friend for a minute, realizing that over the last few weeks, Christine has been distant. They haven't spent time together the way they used to.

"What is going on with you? Are you sure you're not pregnant?"

"No, I'm just tired."

"Well, I've seen you exhausted, but I've never seen you this emotional before. Are you seeing someone?"

"No, I don't have anybody in my life." Verbalizing it makes it seem more real, and Christine can no longer hold back the puddles in her eyes. Tears stream down her face, leaving small tracks in the remains of this morning's make-up. "I'm so sorry, Joanne. I've got to go. It's late, and I'm just really tired." She reaches in her purse and throws some cash on the table. "I'll see you in the morning," she calls over her shoulder as she heads for the door, leaving Joanne bewildered at the table behind her.

The sun disappears beneath the horizon of trees that mark the end of the subdivision as Anna Marie pulls into the drive of every woman's dream home. It should be her dream home, as she designed it herself, clipping pictures from *House Beautiful* while her son napped in the afternoon. All her friends envy her with her granite counter-tops, his-and-hers walk-in closets, and hardwood floors salvaged from a Spanish monastery; but as Anna Marie sits in her driveway, waiting for the garage door to open, she wishes she could give it all back, bend time, and have her family intact. When did it all go wrong? Was it the day Lexi got hurt? Was it even earlier than that? Was it because the house took longer to build, causing Zack and her to argue? If only her friends could see what this beautiful home has cost her. Or was it even deeper than that? Was it because she did not believe that she deserved to have it all? Was she too blessed — having an amazing marriage, two healthy children, a gorgeous home, and money to spare? Did she create this nightmare, somewhere in the dark edges of her mind, that nobody deserved to have it all? Was it that small seed of negativity that gave birth to this nightmare?

She pulls the car into the garage, shuts off the ignition, and grabs her purse from the passenger seat. She slides the key into the side compartment and pulls out the flyer, crumbling the folded paper in her tight grip. Perhaps this will be enough. She unfolds her body from behind the wheel and slams the door behind her.

The door to the garage swings open to reveal the dirty breakfast dishes left on the kitchen counter from earlier this morning and the profile of her husband hunched over a styrofoam serving of chicken soup. He glances in her direction, slurping up the last noodle from his spoon, and nods hello. As Anna Marie makes her way to the adjacent bar stool, she notices the shards of glass are no longer glistening on the tile floor but sitting safely in the dustpan by the trash. She climbs onto the bar stool, slides her hand across his back and rests it on his shoulder.

"Any news about Brian?"

"Nothing," Zack shakes his head.

Look. I'm sorry about this morning." She pauses as Zack's eyes remain focused on the empty container in front of him. "I understand where you are coming from, and I don't want you to leave. I need you, too. I am going to talk to someone."

Zack's neck wrinkles as he turns to face her, his eyes tugging between disbelief and joy.

"I am not ready to talk about Lexi yet. But I found this group..." Anna Marie unfolds the flyer for Dr. Abba's new therapy group to show him, "and I think it's a start. Right?"

"It's a start."

"Would you like to go with me?"

"I need to be out there looking for him not talking about it."

Anna Marie nods her head in silent agreement.

Zack wants to reach out and wrap his arms around her, to comfort her until all of the hurt has gone away, but instead he reaches for the take-out containers, slides off of the stool, and walks to the trashcan.

"We got a letter in the mail today." Zack slides the dustpan containing the glass shards into the trashcan and pulls out the bag, tying the ends firmly shut. "It's about the house."

"What about the house?"

"What do you think, Annie? We are two months behind on the mortgage. We're going to have to sell the house. We can't keep paying for Lexi's hospital bills and the house."

"Are you asking me a question or making a statement?" Anna Marie stomps over to the dirty dishes on the counter, plops them down into the sink, and begins filling up the basin with soapy water. "I don't care if I live in a shack," she says. "I am not going to pull the plug, Zack."

Zack slumps his head. "I never asked you to do that. I don't give a rat's ass about this house; but I do want some kind of quality of our life back. We can't keep living this way."

"I have no life without her."

"No life without her? Annie, what about me? What about Brian? Are we nothing? Lexi is gone. She will never be the same, and at some point we have to accept that, and salvage what is left of our family."

Anna Marie screams at the top of her lungs, "Sell the damn house, Zack! I am never letting her go." She storms out of the room.

Zack hears her heavy footsteps down the hall, and he knows where she is headed. The door to Lexi's room slams shut behind her. Anna Marie falls onto her daughter's made-up bed, grabs her favorite giraffe, curls up into a ball, and weeps.

Her cries can be heard in the kitchen as Zack stares at the pictures on the wall, the happy family he barely remembers staring back at him. His beautiful daughter, her lifeless body lying in a hospital bed 15 minutes away; his son, who has disappeared, with no leads from the police; his wife, stuck in a moment that time can't acknowledge, unable to accept the fact that her family is not the same family that was once in these pictures. With a heavy heart, Zack makes his way to the only locked cabinet in the kitchen and pulls out a bottle of bourbon. He promised years ago that he would never touch the stuff, especially after watching his alcoholic father die from liver failure and disappointment. But life has conspired against him, turning his world upside down. Helpless and sad, Zack turns to the only comfort left, and even that is kept behind lock and key.

————

Securely wrapped in her dirty terry cloth bathrobe, Diane sits at the breakfast table, staring out of the window at the neighbor's cat, Buttons, as he hunts a blue jay with great stealth and agility. She glances at her watch. 9:30. She should be teaching natural science to twenty-eight unruly eighth-graders, but instead she reaches for the open bag of potato chips and grabs a handful. It doesn't matter that she just ate breakfast thirty minutes ago. She has watched fifteen minutes of *The People's Court*, brushed her hair, and observed Animal Planet through her window; she can reward herself. She pops the last chip into her mouth, chewing it slowly the way a cow savors her cud, and contemplates a second handful. Instead, she stands up, wanders aimlessly to the front door, and exits into the blaring light of day.

She shuffles down the front walk, observing the drooping mum leaves.

"You could probably use some water, huh, little flowers? Maybe in a few hours, when it has warmed up a little more out here." Diane pulls the robe tighter around her large form as a cool breeze rustles through her hair and the dead leaves on the ground. Diana prefers fall. It is her favorite season, with its burst of color and soothing coolness. However, now that Ben is absent, the colors don't seem as vibrant, and the cool area just reminds her of how alone she really is. She squints absently at the sun, feeling its warmth, and then glances back at her watch. 9:38.

She shuffles back up the walk and into the house to sit in Ben's recliner. He loves this recliner, the only thing in the house he didn't want to exchange for something new. It is molded perfectly to the contours of his body, visible in his absence like an angel in the snow. Diane doesn't understand the bond Ben has with the chair. To her, it isn't very comfortable, but her larger contours rest on the untamed areas of the recliner; she doesn't experience the same comfort of a worn-out chair or old companion.

Flipping through channels, Diane jumps in the recliner at the sudden ringing of her phone. She reaches for the phone resting comfortably in its cradle on the end table next to her elbow.

"Hello?"

"Hey, Diane. It's Mel. I got your message. How are you holding up?" Diane's friendship with Melanie is the longest running relationship in her life, aside from her marriage to Ben. They met in college in an intro to teaching fundamentals course. Diane continued with her education; but Mel realized her affinity for children didn't translate well in the classroom, and pursued a career in nursing.

"I don't know what to do with myself." Diane glances down at the stains on her unwashed bathrobe.

"It's just a break, right? You'll be back at work before you know it. Have you heard from Ben?"

"No, I haven't. I don't expect to, either. How could I be so blind? I thought we were happy."

"I know, honey. I know."

"Maybe he was bored with me. Maybe I'm too predictable. I just like routine. Is it so awful that I like to eat the same thing on the same day of the week, or that I like sex only on Fridays? I mean, some men never get it."

"Okay, now just stop; I feel really awkward. How do you know he hasn't disappeared like the others?" Melanie stammers.

"Because who would want me or Ben? We have nothing anybody would want. No money, no rich relatives."

"I don't know, but I don't think everyone that is missing has a rich relative. There have to be regular Johns in the mix."

"Stop! I can't imagine Ben being taken. I can deal with him leaving, but I can't handle the idea of him being in trouble."

"I'm sorry. I didn't mean to upset you." Melanie's voice drops off, reaching for something to say to break the uncomfortable silence.

"It's okay, Mel… Honestly, I'm just a hopeless case. I don't even teach well apparently. I have no idea what to do."

"Try the group thing you were telling me about. I think that may be a good start… It could at least get you back into the classroom."

"I know. But, I'd really hate to miss the finale of *Dancing with the Stars*. I've been watching it all season."

"Well, think about it this way. You can't watch *Dancing with the Stars* if you can't pay your cable bill because you no longer have a job."

"Good point."

"Let me know how it goes."

"I will."

"Are you sure you're ok? Do you need me to come over?"

"No. I'll be fine."

"Well, you know where I am if you need me."

Diane lays the cordless down on the table next to her, replaces it with the remote, and searches for another mindless show to occupy her time.

"Christine, good to see you again. Please sit down." Dr. Abba, in his argyle sweater and faded jeans, moves from behind his desk to his traditional chair next to the only window in his office. Christine asked him about it once, why he always chose that particular chair when there were other chairs that looked far more comfortable. He said he liked the natural light the window provided. Natural light always reveals things as they really are.

"I don't *have* joy in my life, so I can't *stop* it," Christine blurts out as she sits down on the edge of her oversized chair. Her legs start to shake, so she jumps up and paces, picking distractedly at her fingernails.

"I'm sorry?"

"You asked me about joy. I just don't have it!" Christine throws her hands in the air and rests them on the top of her head.

"Oh. I see." Dr. Abba's calm voice seems out of place following Christine's rant. "Although that's not what you told me. You told me you felt joy when you heard the baby's heart beat."

"So what? Joy also causes me pain."

"Only because you stop the joy. Because your fear is so great, you don't allow room for joy to grow in your life."

"How do you know this baby will bring me joy?"

"How do you know that the baby won't? There are no guarantees in life; but I will tell you, no one has ever regretted having a baby in my practice. Honestly, it's always been the reverse, in my experience."

"I can't do it. I can't take that chance."

"All I ask is that you take some time and ask your heart to guide you. Just see how things unfold. In the end, you will know what's right for you."

"I have, and I did! I want the procedure tomorrow."

"Very well, then I'll tell Dr. Windsor you are able to make a sound decision."

"You think I'm a monster, don't you?"

"Quite the contrary. I think you are blessed. There is no judgment here. You must find your own truth, and everyone's truth is different."

"But I can still come to the group, right?"

"Is your mother still missing? The mother you never seem to mention?" He raises his eyebrows at her.

Taken aback by the sarcasm, Christine whispers, "Uh, yes, of course."

"Then I'll see you in a couple of weeks. Take care of yourself, Christine. Allow yourself to feel the joy in life."

"Eventually, I hope I will, Dr. Abba. Thanks for signing off on me." Her voice softens, almost betraying a vulnerability that she tries to keep hidden in the dark unreachable space in her heart. Christine's mouth opens as if to say something else; but her mind cuts her heart off, and the moment and the thought are lost. "Thanks again," she repeats, and slips out of the office, leaving a world of possibilities behind her.

Exiting the office building, Christine turns left and merges with the hordes of hurried people with places to go and things to do. She clings to the periphery, moving at a slower pace and remembering when she was one of those people. She has always been in a hurry to get the story, climbing over whomever she had to in order to get to the top. Dr. Abba's words slip uninvited into her mind, hijacking her train of thoughts and changing its direction.

She catches a glimpse of her reflection in the Mrs. Fields' Cookie Shop window and turns to stare. "Who are you?" The words escape her lips before her mind can stop them. As she stares into her translucent reflection, she feels older, seeing the worry-lines forming across her forehead and beside her eyes accentuated by the shadows of the sun. She stopped running a week ago, unable to focus on anything for an extended period of time; anything that is, except the unwanted baby taking over her body and the unknowing father lurking in the shadows of her mind. Six months ago, she never would have dreamed this is where she would be: lying, unhappy, and out of control. "Tomorrow. This will all be over tomorrow." Unable to find comfort in this thought or any answers in her transparent likeness, she enters the cookie shop with the ringing of the door chime in her ear.

Like an alcoholic on a binge, she snatches up two hot chocolate chip cookies and a fresh cinnamon raisin, tossing them into a paper bag. Christine makes her way to the cooler and grabs a half-pint of milk to go with them before heading to the register.

"Did you find everything you needed?" The cashier glances at her out of the corners of her eyes. She has seen people impatient to satisfy some sinful need for chocolate before, but this seems like more than that.

"Yes, thanks." Christine taps the corner of her credit card on the counter.

"That will be $8.11."

Christine hands her card to the cashier and, in its absence, begins tapping her fingers.

"I know it is none of my business, but are you okay?"

"You're right – it is none –" and then she stops herself, knowing it's not her fault she's miserable, and responds, "I'm fine." Christine returns her credit card to her wallet and her wallet to her purse. She snatches the milk and cookies from the counter and spots a bench in front of the store.

Devouring the first chocolate chip cookie from the bag, she breathes in deeply, sucking up the smog hovering above her head. Her phone breaks her trance of the smooth, silky milk chocolate morsels dissolving in her mouth. "What now?" Christine shouts to the hurried crowd streaming in front of her. She pulls her phone from her coat pocket.

Recognizing Joanne's number, she decides to answer it. "Yes?"

"Where are you?"

"I'm sitting on a bench eating chocolate chips cookies. Where are you?"

"Oh my god, you are having a nervous breakdown. You are, aren't you?"

"Really, you think?"

"Maybe you should go see this therapist privately."

"Great, even you think I need a shrink now."

"Well, I just call it like I see it. I'm in the office. Just wondering when you might grace us with your presence." Christine can hear the joviality in her mocking, but she feels her cheeks grow hot in spite of it.

"I'll be there in fifteen."

"Hey. . .what kind of cookies?"

"Mrs. Fields."

"Could you grab me one?"

"Sure."

"And coffee?"

"No problem."

"I think I like you better when you're at your wits' end - you're very agreeable."

"I know, right? Don't get used to it."

Her phone beeps, letting her know she has a message. Christine hangs up with Joanne and listens to her messages.

"Hi, Christine. This is Dr. Windsor's assistant. Unfortunately, Dr. Windsor needs to reschedule all her appointments for tomorrow as well as next week. She has been subpoenaed to appear in court and doesn't know for sure how long she will be out of the office. Please call the office back to reschedule. We apologize for any inconvenience."

Christine slams her phone down onto the wooden bench. "This is not happening to me! This is a conspiracy!"

A group of women gliding past shake their heads at the crazy outburst, their faces contorted into a look of disdain.

"I suppose *Dr. Abba* would call this a sign," she bellows " but *I* call it a freaking NIGHTMARE!" People begin to stop and watch as Christine throws her head back and releases a scream into the universe. They continue to stare as Christine picks up her phone, shoves the dislodged battery back into place, and punches a series of numbers. "Yes, this is Christine Becker. I can't believe this is happening to me. When can we get this over with?" Christine tries to control her anger, but it is dripping on every word.

"I'm so sorry we have to change your appointment." Patty's molasses drawl flows painfully through the phone and into Christine's ear. "It looks like she is three weeks out... will that work?"

"Of course. NO, THAT WON'T WORK!" Christine's voice cracks under the force of her anger.

"I'm so sorry, ma'am. We are trying our best to work everyone in. That is the best we can do, unless, of course, there is a cancellation."

"This is ridiculous!" Christine shouts into the phone. "Can you give me a referral for another doctor?"

"I can, but as a new patient, the chances that you will get a consultation and then book the procedure before three weeks is going to be extremely difficult."

"Thank you, Scarlett O'Hara. I'll take my chances."

The syrupy voice alters slightly on the other end but maintains its Southern sweetness. "You can try Dr. Galvin at 212-555-0989 or Dr. Felder at 212-555-9830."

"Thanks." Without a goodbye, Christine hangs up. With new numbers, she calms herself enough to sit back down on the bench and dials the first number.

"Hi, I would like to make an appointment with Dr. Galvin."

"Has Dr. Galvin seen you before?"

"No."

"I'm sorry, but Dr. Galvin is no longer accepting new patients."

"Thanks!" She once again hangs up the phone and calls the other number.

"Hi, I would like to make a new patient appointment with Dr. Felder."

"Sure. Do you have a referral?"

"Yes, Dr. Windsor's office. I can get paperwork if needed."

"That's fine. Not a problem. Let me see..."

"Finally." Christine whispered to herself.

"Dr. Felder's next available appointment is January 15th."

"January 15? That's two months away. What the hell's wrong with you people?"

Christine stands up and begins to pace, running one hand through her hair and holding the phone to her ear with the other.

"Excuse me?"

"I just need to get an appointment. How hard can that be? At this rate, I'll give birth before I can abort it."

"I apologize, but I can put you on our cancellation list."

"No, thanks."

Defeated, she once again dials Dr. Windsor's office. "You were right. I'll take the appointment for three weeks out."

"I'm sorry, but that slot has been filled. The next possible date is in four weeks." There is a hint of satisfaction in the receptionist's voice.

"Fine, just put me down. But *please* call me if anything opens up."

"Absolutely, and we are so sorry for the inconvenience. Thank you so much."

Christine grunts back into the phone.

"Hold, please."

Christine enjoys the silence as she waits.

"I just spoke with Dr. Windsor, and she has requested that you come in for a check-up at least two weeks prior to the surgery, just to make sure everything is good to go for the procedure. You will be almost fourteen weeks pregnant by that time."

"Thanks for reminding me. If she can see me for an appointment, then why can't she go ahead and do the surgery?"

A small giggle escapes the receptionist's lips. Christine can tell her pain is giving her great pleasure. "Oh, you won't see Dr. Windsor when you come in. You'll only see the nurse practitioner."

"Fine. Whatever."

"Is there a specific day you like to come in?"

"Whenever."

"How about three weeks from Wednesday at 10:00 a.m.?"

"Just perfect!"

Jesse rolls onto his side and folds his pillow up to cover his ears. Despite the extra fluff and fabric, he can still hear Kevin stumbling around his empty apartment, breaking lamps and picture frames as he bumps into tables and walls. Jesse was also repeatedly disturbed throughout the night with Kevin's drunken rantings as he shouted at God, angry over his slighted portion.

Jesse sits up in bed and scratches his scalp with his fingers. For the past two weeks, Jesse has gotten little sleep, only a couple hours in the early morning when Kevin finally passes out and falls into a deep sleep. "This has got to stop," Jesse thinks as he collapses back into his pillows. He lies awake, staring at the ceiling and concocting a plan to get him to the first group session tomorrow. He knows that Kevin will never go on his own; but it's the only way he can think of to get some sleep.

"Can I help you?" Kevin's ruffled figure looms in the doorway.

Jesse smiles warmly, "Actually, I'm supposed to lead a group session on the other side of town, but my car won't start. I was hoping that you might be willing to drive me, hang around for an hour or so, and then bring me home."

"I don't know," Kevin replies. "Not exactly how I want to spend my Thursday night."

Jesse hangs his head.

"Fine, I'll do it. I need to go by the store for beer anyway."

"Okay! Great! Thanks, man."

Jesse waits outside for Kevin to get dressed. A few minutes later, he emerges from the apartment. "Let's roll, emo man."

"You know, Kevin, you just might find this meeting interesting." Jesse sits in the passenger seat, the crinkle of beer cans under his feet.

"Oh, really? Why's that?"

"It's a support group for people who have had loved ones disappear. Maybe they can give you some insight as to whether Kate has disappeared like the others. Why don't you join us?"

"I don't think so. I prefer to deal with things in my own way."

"You mean by drinking so much that you pass out? That's not going to help you deal with things. You're just avoiding it and digging your own grave in the process."

"Fine. If it gets you off my back, I'll sit. But don't expect anything."

Jesse arranges some comfortable chairs and couches into a circle. Kevin picks his seat at the far end and plops down, waiting for time to pass. Laura Windsor enters next, greeting her old colleague with a warm hug, and sits apprehensively down opposite Kevin. Anna Marie and Diane arrive at the same time, neither one excited about what is to come. Christine is the last one in, unable to be anywhere on time these days. Laura shifts in her seat uncomfortably.

"Hello, Christine. I didn't realize you had a missing loved-one."

"Oh... yeah. Who's missing in your life, Dr. Windsor?"

"Please, call me Laura."

Jesse shuts the door behind him, interrupting their conversation. "Okay. Let's get started. First, I am honored to have you all here, and I want this to be a place where you can be honest, voice any fears, sadness, hopes, and dreams." He takes the remaining seat next to Anna Marie.

"Let's get to know each other a little better. Why don't you tell everyone why you are here? Why don't we start with you? Anna Marie, right?"

"That's right. My name is Anna Marie, and my son is missing. It has caused a struggle in my marriage."

Jesse motions to Diane to go next.

"Hello. I'm Diane, and my husband is missing. It has caused problems at work, and I have to be here in order to keep my job."

"Thank you for your honesty, Diane. What about you, Laura?"

"Oh... okay. My name is Laura Windsor. My dog is missing, and I am just beside myself."

Unable to take anymore, Kevin throws his arms up, "You have to be kidding me."

"Kevin, please." Dr. Abba whispers. Slouching down into his chair and folding his arms across his chest, Kevin nods in agreement.

"Let's continue. What about you, Christine?"

"I'm Christine Becker. My mother is missing, and I thought it would be nice to share with others who are going through the same thing."

Laura's brow furrow slightly. "You never mentioned that your mom was missing."

Christine swallows hard. "Uh... it just happened. And I've had a lot going on lately, as you well know."

Jesse cuts his eyes towards Christine; a smile waxes onto his face and quickly wanes.

"And you, Kevin?" Dr. Abba focuses his attention onto his neighbor.

"You said you needed a ride, and I have to stay to take you home. But, honestly, I'm feeling like you set me up."

Jesse shakes his head. Then he says to the group, "Yes, that is why you are physically here, but what brought you to this place in your life?"

Jesse looks around the circle and is greeted only by blank faces. "Anybody? ... No? ... Okay, how about this? If you could pick one word to describe how you are feeling right now, what would it be?"

Before thinking, Diana blurts out, "Abandoned."

Laura follows, "Lonely."

"What about you, Christine?"

"Confused."

"Anna Marie?"

"Heartbroken."

Kevin, sitting next to Anna Marie, smiles and says, "Hungry."

Everyone looks at him.

"Well, I am! I didn't get a chance to eat dinner before I was asked to be a taxi service."

Still stinging from his crass response to her missing dog, Laura raises her hand.

"Yes, Laura?"

"Why is he in this group?"

As if in response, Christine's phone rings in its short, sharp tones.

"Excuse me. I am so sorry." Christine reaches for her phone and silences it.

"I thought you were supposed to LISTEN in therapy. He NEEDED a ride." Kevin absently rubs the back of his neck.

"Please, Kevin. I think it would help if you shared what's going on in your life." Jesse leans forward in his seat.

Everyone sits in silence waiting for him to speak. Kevin moves from side to side in his seat until the absence of sound gets the best of him.

"Fine," Kevin blurts. "My wife is missing, but I don't think she's missing like the others. I think she chose to leave me."

The faces staring at him soften, and Laura slumps in her chair, thinking to herself that she can understand why.

"And how does that make you feel?" Jesse asks.

Kevin leans forward resting his elbow on his thighs, and hangs his head. The silence is almost suffocating again, but his voice finally releases the tensions.

"Regretful."

Diane shakes her head in agreement, "I feel that way, too."

"What way?" Jesse focuses his attention on her round face.

"I feel like my husband left by his own accord. He isn't really missing. He just doesn't want to be with me anymore."

Anna Marie speaks up, "I think my son did the same thing."

The room grows quiet, each member processing what has been shared. Christine's phone vibrates again, interrupting their silent thoughts.

"Would you mind shutting your phone off? It helps if everyone can stay in the moment." Jesse leans to rest against the back of the chair and addresses the group. "Why do you think they wanted to leave?"

"Because I was an ass," Kevin interjects immediately.

Diana divulges, "Because everyone always leaves."

"Anna Marie, what about you?"

Tears well in her eyes and flow down her face. As she buries her face in her hands, she sobs, "Because I'm a horrible mother."

———

A cold breeze blows through the trees and ruffles the autumn-hued leaves, sending a few cascading down to rest on the pavement. Christine wraps her shawl snuggly around her body as she walks beside Joanne. The soft glow emanating from the street lamps breaks through the branches and falls weightlessly on their faces.

Christine stops and turns to face Joanne. "So are you going to tell me what's so important? You called me three times in an hour! You knew I was in the middle of a group session. I can't exactly answer the phone." Christine throws her hands up into the dark night, her forehead scrunched with frustration.

"Sorry," Joanne folds her arms across her chest, pushing her hip to the side. "I just thought you might want to know that while you were busy spying on a therapy session, they found the regime leader who has the president's daughter."

"What? Where?" Christine's brow relaxes, while her eyes bulge with excitement.

"The military has his compound surrounded, and the president wants him taken out alive."

The gears of Christine's mind churn, flooding her brain with information. "Who do you think they'll give the assignment to?"

Christine's eyes shine with a glint of hope, pleading Joanne to mouth the words she wants to hear.

"Simon." Joanne looks down, unable to watch disappointment swallow Christine's body.

"That is SO unfair!" Christine's shoulders drop with the weight of her words. She shudders as the cold seeps through her wool shawl and clothes to the skin and bones beneath.

"Well, to be honest, it's not like you've been around much lately. And when you are, you are still somewhere else."

Christine's mouth opens slightly, allowing the sting to settle into a nice burn; but what can she say in her own defense? Deep down she knows the truth of Joanne's words, the words only a friend could utter; so she nods.

"Let's talk about something else. You're tired, and there is nothing we can do about it tonight." Joanne slips her arm through the sliver of space between Christine's body and arm, linking the two together. She rests her head briefly on Christine's shoulder as they walk, dried leaves crunching beneath their steps. "How was your first shrink session?

"There was a bunch of feelings and crying. It's so weird, but at least I'll be able to get more of a sequential time line behind the disappearances, if the therapist would move past all this feelings crap. Why would anyone ever go to therapy?"

Anna Marie fades into the darkness as she emerges from the fluorescent residue emanating from the hospital windows. After acknowledging the unbearable truth in the group session, she felt an indescribable urge to visit Lexi before heading home. There was no change, but it felt good to brush her hair, stroke her face, tuck her in, and kiss her sweet baby girl goodnight. Now, as she walks back to her car, the darkness frees her. Her face drags, her drained eyes puffy from lack of sleep. She collapses into the driver's seat and throws her head back to rest on the headrest. Anna Marie closes her eyes, wallowing in the silence, before inserting the key in the ignition and cranking the car.

The drive home is lonely and quiet except for the occasional passing car. The soft glow from the living room window of her home comforts Anna Marie as she pulls into the driveway. Entering the house, she finds her husband sitting at the dining room table, his hair as disheveled as the stacks of papers on the table in front of him.

"Hey, honey." She walks up behind him and kisses him softy on the crown of his head as she takes off her coat and places it on the bar next to the table.

Zack continues to shuffle papers and presses keys on the calculator sitting at his fingertips. "How did it go?"

"Okay, I guess. I'm worn out. Any news about Brian?" Zack shakes his head from side to side.

"He'll come back. I just know he will," Anna Marie says convincingly unable to consider the alternative.

"And what if those terrorist have him like the others?" Zack snaps back.

"Stop it, don't say things like that," Anna Marie pleads. "He's just mad at me. He'll come back." She gathers her coat and purse as she heads for the bedroom. Although she hasn't slept in their bed for almost a year, she still keeps her clothes beside her husband's in the extravagant walk-in closet. She reaches for one of his shirts and holds it to her face. Breathing in deeply, she absorbs the familiar scent of her husband, and her mind flashes back to a night several years ago, the night Lexi had been conceived.

Anna Marie, Zack and Brian had taken an impromptu trip to the beach, something they never did. After spending all day in the sand and sun, Brian went down easily for the night. Anna Marie and Zack moved to the balcony to enjoy the cool breeze that moved off the coast, and to hear the rhythmic undulation of the waves as they crashed on the shore. Lying next to him, resting her head against his chest, she never felt happier, more content, than in that moment.

As she looks back, that moment becomes even more special because it gave them Lexi. Tears stream down Anna Marie's face as she buries it into her husband's shirt. Oh, to feel his arms around her again! She undresses, leaving her clothes haphazardly on the floor, and then covers her body with a set of flannels, ready to crawl into Lexi's bed and succumb to a world to which only sleep can take her.

Standing in the doorway, Anna Marie calls quietly to her husband, "Hold me...please."

Zack looks up from the tiny print of the bills in front of him. His glasses perch on the tip of his nose. He tilts his head to the side, confused by her unexpected request; but without speaking, he stands up from his chair. Anna Marie reaches out to grab his hand as he walks toward her. She leads him into Lexi's bedroom, and they both crawl into the small twin bed. She rests her head against his chest for the first time in months, breathing in his scent and feeling his warmth. They lay tangled together, waiting for sleep to come and dry their silent tears.

There are several flyers already posted on the telephone pole as Laura Windsor approaches with her newly printed stack of papers with "missing" in bold capital letters. There is one for a yard sale and for an upcoming concert, but the rest are heartbreaking. A small part of her, a very tiny part of her brain, feels embarrassed for posting the panting image of Max next to the smiling faces of a young man by the name of Daniel Brown, a grandmother type named Abigail Thomas, and a little girl no more than six named Emily Flint. Laura shakes her head as she stares into the photocopied images of the missing. "Where did everyone go?" she whispers, more mouthing the worlds than giving them voice.

"Morning, Laura. Any luck finding Max?" Mrs. Evans, the neighborhood gossip, is out for her usual morning walk, catching up on any news she might have missed.

Lost in the little girl's face, Laura jumps at the sound of her voice. She glances over her shoulder to see the frail little woman with silvery white hair coming up the walk. "No, unfortunately. That's why I'm out with more flyers." Dr. Windsor holds a stack of flyers up for her to see.

"If you want, I can pass some out on my walk."

Laura has never really cared much for Mrs. Evans, always prying into her personal life or commenting on the lack thereof, but she can't turn down the help. "I would really appreciate that, Mrs. Evans. How is Mr. Evans?"

"Dying, but aren't we all." Mrs. Evans flashes a broad smile at Laura, then focuses her attention on the stack of flyers. Mrs. Evans has never cared much for Max, always barking and growling at her; he even chased her down the street once after she had cooked bacon for her husband, Ralph. It is her duty to know the comings and goings of the neighborhood, and curiosity always gets the better of her, despite its killing of cats. "I see you have raised the reward to $1500. That does sweeten the pot."

"Well, it couldn't hurt, right?" Laura shifts the flyers and tape in her arms. "Thanks again, Mrs. Evans. If you hear anything. . .;" but Mrs. Evans is already a block away, looking for more neighbors and gossip to procure.

The following Thursday, Dr. Jesse Abba once again knocks on Kevin's door. As he glances up and down the hall, he can hear Kevin stumbling around behind the un-insulated walls of the cheap apartment building. Jesse finally hears Kevin's steps grow louder as they approach the doorway, and he turns to face him as he appears from behind the door.

"Hey, Kevin. I still haven't been able to get the car fixed. It needs a part on backorder or something." Jesse offers a toss of his hand and scrunches his face. "Do you think you could take me again this week?"

Kevin rolls his eyes as he leans against the doorframe. "Yeah… Sure… Whatever." He snatches the keys from the hook by the door and checks his back pocket for his wallet. "Let's go."

Creatures of habit, the group members trickle into the sparsely furnished office and return to their claimed seats, a pseudo home where one searches for the truth.

"Glad everyone could make it. Good to see all of you." Jesse closes the door behind him and walks over to a table in the corner to pour a cup of coffee. "I'd like to work on some of those feelings that came up last session." He glides back to his chair and balances his hot coffee with his notepad and pencil. "What is underneath those feelings when you think about them? Is it that the people have disappeared, or is something much deeper, the real root cause?" Dr. Abba skims over each face, letting the series of questions sink in.

"Laura, let's investigate your loneliness. Where does that stem from?" Jesse leans back into his chair and perches an ankle carefully on his knee. He takes a sip of coffee.

"I miss Max."

The room is filled with silence as Jesse waits for Laura to elaborate. The sound of a lost fly beating against the windowpane echoes throughout the empty space. Laura sits erect in her chair, lips pursed tightly and eyes focused on the design in the carpet.

"Well, that's understandable," Jesse prods. "Tell us a little more."

Laura glances at Jesse's relaxed form. "I understand how it's trivial to some people," her eyes dart quickly to Kevin, who stares absently at the ceiling, "but Max is all I have. Max has always been something I can count on. I'm sad to think he's out there somewhere all alone, no place to sleep, eating garbage."

"And so on an immediate level, you are lonely because you are separated from Max; but would you say, on a deeper level, you feel lonely in your life? In your free time? In general?"

Laura shifts in her seat and glances around at the blurry faces staring at her. She swallows hard, and in the quiet, she feels as if the sound reverberates throughout the circle. "Uh, no. I don't need anyone except Max."

"You don't let anyone into your life besides Max?" Jesse releases his leg to the floor and leans forward, holding his pencil to his lips.

"I don't need close relationships in my personal life. It's my choice. I see people all day long. What I want is to figure out what happened to Max. Why are all these people disappearing? Are they dead? And is there even hope of seeing Max again?"

"I agree with Dr. Windsor... I mean Laura. I think we should discuss why these people are missing, and if there's any connection," Christine interjects, her face glowing with excitement and anticipation. Jesse raises his eyebrow at Christine. Aware of the confused faces staring at her, Christine quickly continues, "Because I want to get my mother back. I miss her." Christine darts her eyes toward each face, willing them to believe her. Her eyes meet Jesse's, revealing a knowing face that Christine pretends not to see.

"We are doing that through this process," Jesse continues, "so you will have to trust me. Now, Christine, in our last session, you said you were confused?"

"Yes, and I think we both know why and I would prefer not to share it with the group."

"I was referring to your mother. What makes you confused about your mother?"

"Oh, right. I am confused because I don't know... I mean... understand why they would take her."

Letting her off the hook, Jesse shifts his attention to Anna Marie.

"Anna Marie, why don't you share with us your feelings of being broken-hearted?"

"Well, I'm heartbroken that my family is falling apart. Everything has shattered around me. I'm devastated that the people I love the most I can't hug, kiss, or tuck into bed. What hurts the most is that I don't get to hear her sweet little voice anymore."

Kevin interjects, "I thought your boy was missing."

"He is." Anna Marie's face turns up in confusion with a slight hint of frustration. Kevin holds his finger to his head, twirling it for effect beside his temple, and mouths the word "crazy" in Dr. Abba's direction.

Jesse returns his gesture with a stern look. "Kevin."

"What?" He snaps defensively. "She called him a she, not a he."

"Kevin, I called on you to share about your regret, not her pronoun choice. And please, let's keep our comments to ourselves unless we think they are useful to the whole group."

"Fine." Kevin crosses his arms across his chest.

"What do you regret?" Jesse asks again.

"I regret coming here," Kevin smiles.

Jesse locks eyes with him until he feels totally uncomfortable. "OK, I regret not telling her the truth," Kevin says. "And not opening up to her like I use to about everything. Actually, I regret most of the choices that I made for the last three years."

Relieved that Kevin is attempting to participate, Jesse doesn't push the envelope and places his focus on Diane. "Diane, what makes you feel abandoned?"

"I feel abandoned because I don't believe he's missing. I think he just left, and people are just trying to make me believe he's missing because it's less painful. It was a perfect time to cover his tracks. But that's how it happens, right? Everyone always leaves in the end."

"What do you mean?"

"You can't trust anyone. My own father didn't even step up and if that wasn't hard enough God took my mother too." Her words turn into inaudible mumbling as sobs take their place. Dr. Abba reaches around behind him for the box of tissues and hands them to her. She pulls a few from the box.

"This is ridiculous. I thought therapy was supposed to make you feel better." Kevin shifts uncomfortably in his chair. "Every time we come here, someone starts crying."

"Sometimes, Kevin, we must walk through the dark to get to the light." Jesse says softly.

"What is that supposed to mean?"

"Just think about it; eventually you will understand."

Kevin responds by rolling his eyes.

———

Bracing her heel with the other foot, Diane kicks off her white stained tennis shoes, leaving them in the hallway by the door. Hours before, she had admired Christine's designer heels, but her feet are too large and carry too much weight for anything so reckless and sexy. Diane ponders them as they lie on the floor. "Perhaps Ben would have stayed if I had traded you in for shoes like hers," Diane mumbles to her worn-out shoes. Quickly burying the thought, she walks barefoot to the kitchen to pop a frozen pizza into the oven. The neon green numbers on the oven clock remind her that it's time for *America's Got Talent*, so she sets the timer, shuffles into the living room, and lowers herself into her husband's recliner. She reaches for the remote and puts in the numbers for the memorized channel. However, instead of discovering the laughable antics of the judges, she finds herself staring to the familiar visage of the President of the United States. Frustrated, she flips through the channels but finds only his stern features on every channel.

"It gives me great pleasure to announce that as a result of the swift actions of the US military, the people responsible for these horrible acts have been apprehended. They will stand trial. If they are found guilty and fail to disclose the whereabouts of all missing Americans, including my daughter Grace, they will be publicly executed before the people of the United States of America."

As the President continues his worldwide broadcast, Diane hears the alarming decibels of the timer. Eager to get back to the television to hear the closing remarks, she hurries to the kitchen and returns with the hot pizza, a bottle of Coke, and on a whim, a package of Oreo cookies. She settles back into the recliner, and begins eating the mixture of bread, tomato sauce, and melted cheese directly from the metal tray, following it with a Coca-Cola chaser.

Entranced by the scene before her, Diane consumes mouthful after mouthful of food.

"The American people deserve justice. And with God as my witness, they will get it." The President's lips remain firmly pressed as he glares into the camera, daring anyone to sway him from what he must do.

Realizing she has eaten the last of the Oreos, Diane licks each finger, careful to retrieve every crumb.

⸻

After a difficult day, Dr. Windsor longs for the bowl of leftover pasta in her refrigerator, a glass of Cabernet and the solitude of her private courtyard. As the cab driver heads down Columbus Avenue towards West 84th Street, where Dr. Windsor resides, she shrieks to the driver, "Stop the cab." The cabbie responds by slamming on his brakes, sending her face two millimeters away from the glass partition as he jerks the cab over to the curb. Dr. Windsor, undaunted by the driver's recklessness, keeps her eyes glued to the sight before her. She throws him a twenty and exits the cab without her change, a block before her intended destination. Hopeful, she begins frantically searching for Max in a long line of impostors, each person holding a chocolate lab by a leash as they try to convince her that their dog is her prized puppy. Her brows furrow, as Max is not among the menagerie of scam artists, so she makes her way to her two-story brownstone.

"Dr. Laura Windsor?" shouts a young man running up the street, proffering a new dog for inspection.

"Who wants to know?" Dr. Windsor sneers as she glances over her shoulder at him with the dog that is definitely not her Max. She can tell by the white spot on his tail. She digs in her purse for her keys.

"I found your dog – the one on the reward poster."

"Really?"

"I found your dog. It's Max, right?"

"That is not Max." Laura snaps as she glances back down the street. "It's about the money, isn't it? Isn't it?!" Rage consumes her.

"Get out of here! ALL OF YOU!" For emphasis, she walks over to the light post in front of her apartment and rips down the poster of Max. "You're sick! You're all sick."

Unable to keep hot, angry tears from streaming down her face, Dr. Windsor struggles to unlock her front door and slams it shut behind her.

———

Over the last two weeks, Christine has sat at her desk, researching everyone who has been reported missing in the last few months, looking for links to the chain. Although she should be focusing on the arrested terrorists, something just doesn't seem right to her. Why would terrorists abduct random Americans? She could understand kidnapping the president's daughter, but random people that no one but their loved ones would miss? There has to be more to it. Despite her keeping busy, in the dark corners of her mind looms the unborn baby, moving, growing inside of her, and now she once again sits in the examination room, confronting a truth she has desperately tried to ignore.

"Good morning, Christine." The assistant smiles.

"It will be better once this is over." Christine leans back on the table.

"Oh, now, this is exciting. You get to see your baby." The assistant grabs the tube of gel and the ultrasound wand. "This is going to feel cold."

Christine's body cringes in anticipation of the cold gel falling onto her bare belly, a little paunch that is hardly visible under her loose shirt. The young assistant carefully runs the wand across Christine's belly, stopping occasionally to capture images for the doctor to review. Christine turns her head away from the monitor, unwilling to look at the little human moving around on the screen.

"Everything looks great, Ms. Becker. The baby is right on track. Would you like to know the sex?"

"No."

"Well, then, let me print a few of these, and you'll be good to go."

"Great," Christine mutters to the wall.

The doctor's assistant places a thin stack of black-and-whites on the counter. "You're good until next time, Ms. Becker. You can finish up at the counter when you are ready. Take your time."

Christine doesn't even wait for the assistant to leave before gathering her belongings from the chair beside the table and leaving. As Christine hurries out of the office, she hears her name being screeched behind her.

"Ms. Becker! Ms. Becker!"

"What?" Christine turns around to find the assistant jogging toward her, the black and white pictures in her hand.

"Ms. Becker, I am glad I caught you. You forgot your pictures! The father-to-be might want to see those, you know." The assistant winks, then returns to her stack of files and her next patient.

Christine shoves the pictures into her purse, catching a slight glimpse of a possible arm in doing so. She pulls them back out. The little image outlines a tiny form with its arms behind its head as though it was on a hammock. Tears stream down her face as she takes in the beautiful image. Shoving the pictures into her purse, she speaks softly to herself, "Why are you doing this to me?" She looks up with traces of tears still visible on her cheeks. When she reaches the counter to finalize payment, the office assistant notices her state and offers her some water. She declines, signs the voucher, and exits the office.

———◆———

Jessie knocks on Kevin's door.

"I'm not driving. You are," Kevin says. "I know your car is fine. If you get off by dragging me to these things, just know I think you're the one who needs help. Nonetheless, I'll go since we both know the alternative isn't working."

Kevin gets his coat.

The usuals trickle in, finding their seats. The room smells of freshly brewed coffee and dampness. The last few days have been cold and wet, and in such a drafty building, the heat can't keep up, allowing the moisture to seep through the brick walls and into the room and bones behind it.

Jesse begins, "Is there anything you want to discuss? Anything that you may have thought of since last week?"

In the silence that follows, the door groans open as Christine rushes in.

"Sorry. Sorry." Christine tiptoes to her seat and quietly sets her bag on the floor at her feet.

"Glad you could join us, Christine." Jesse turns to look at her. "We were just getting started. I asked if there was something anyone wanted to discuss."

Again, silence fills the room, except for the last gurgle of coffee as the last drops spit out into the pot below.

"Okay. In that case, I would like you to all go a little bit deeper, deeper than you have ever allowed yourselves to go before, so deep that fear will try to stop you. Because the pain is so great you feel it will consume you."

Kevin shifts in his chair. "That sounds unpleasant. Why would anyone EVER want to go HERE?"

"Because that's where the healing takes place. When we face our pain, when we acknowledge the void, when we grieve our losses, we allow the past to stay in the past; but when you lug it around, you hold it in the present moment. You carry it with you, allowing it to weigh you down." Jesse looks around at the gathered group, avoiding his glance. "Laura, let's start with you. In the deepest part of your being, what experience made you choose the word 'loneliness'?"

"What does this have to do with bringing Max back?" Laura looks at Dr. Abba with wild, wide eyes.

"We have no control over when and if Max or the people who are missing will return. But we do have control over how we will react to the outcome, and the best way I've seen for people to work through distress is when they work on being whole without the wounds. When you risk going deep, there is always a gift on the other end."

"Fine. The first time I can remember being lonely was at boarding school."

"And why were you at boarding school?"

Laura crosses and re-crosses her legs. "My mom thought it would be a good idea."

"Why did she think that?"

Taking a deep breath, Laura speaks aloud the burden she has spoken of only once before. "Because I told her that her new boyfriend was touching me; and either she didn't believed me or that was her way of keeping me safe."

"That must have been very hard on you." Jesse leans forward in his chair, his somber face willing her to continue.

Laura attempts a nervous laugh. "Why would that be hard on me? Because my family was shattered? Because my dad was dead from a heart attack, and my mother was so pathetic she would prefer to be with a child molester than to raise her own daughter? Because I've spent every Christmas alone since then?" Laura's eyes puddle with unshed tears. She wipes them away with a brush of her finger. "I was devastated after my dad's death. I was numb after he was gone. It didn't help that his memories were everywhere. If I went to school, I remembered the conversations we had on the ride there. If I rode my horse, I remembered how patient he was when he taught me to ride. At the store, I thought about the little surprises he would bring, a box of animal crackers or a piece of candy. I desperately clung to any thread of a family existence, and she sent me away. How could she do that? How could she send me away from my horse, away from my home, away from my friends at school for some guy she hardly knew? Some guy that could do what he did? So 'lonely' actually doesn't even truly describe it. I stopped living, frozen in time. I suppose I still am. The other girls at the boarding school made fun of me because I was a loner. I buried myself in my schoolwork. When Christmas came around, I made up excuses not to go home. Soon my mom stopped asking. When I turned 21, I got my inheritance from my father that he had specifically set aside for me. After that, I've never looked back." She wipes away a tear attempting to escape down her cheek. She clears her throat. "Do you want to hear something funny? More than 15 people tried to convince me that their dog was my dog. What kind of people would sell their dog for money? Show me the gift in that."

Jesse leans back to retrieve a tissue from his desk. "The gift, Laura, is that by slowly realizing that not all people are bad, the good people will begin to gravitate towards you, and then you can experience love in all areas of your life."

"Not in this lifetime," she responds, crossing her arms tightly across her chest, her face sternly set staring out of the window into the darkness beyond.

Jesse writes down a few notes to review later. He then turns his attention to Diane, who is attempting to locate a package of tissues from the oversized bag on her lap. "What about you, Diane?"

Diane's eyes bulge like a startled animal discovered in the night. She has known that this time would come, but that doesn't make her feel any more at ease. Wiping a tear from her eyes with the located tissue, she turns to Laura. "Well, it sounds like your dad was just wonderful. I always dreamed my dad would show up one day and do all those things. Not so much because I missed him; I never knew him. But it would have made things easier on my mom." She sighs, "My mom did everything for me and worked nights, too. She would work all night and then show up at every play, teacher's conference, recital, and soccer game. My mother was everything to me. She often said we were two peas in a pod; where I was, she'd be. I think she felt bad that I never had a father, so she did her best to make up for it. Then when I was 12 years old," Diane wipes another tear from her eye, "My mother tucked me into bed after reading *The Hobbit* with me. We always read before bedtime, or we would make up rhymes of our own and laugh until it hurt. Then, like every other night, she closed my door saying, 'Sweet dreams my little angel, I will see you in the morning light.'

Then, just like every night, she left for work. I wish I would have known then how much she sacrificed for me. I wish I could tell her what an amazing mother she was." Diane lowers her head and attempts to discreetly wipe away the tears streaming down her face.

"But that evening was different. That night she switched shifts to help someone out, so our neighbor came over to stay with me. She did that once or twice a month to help my mom out when my normal sitter had plans. I'm sure she knew how much my mom had to juggle, and it was her way of helping out. Mom switched to the graveyard shift. And that's exactly what happened, when all was said and done." Like a wave, Diane's face waxes irritation, anger. Her lips purse tightly and her cheeks flush. "Some pothead teenager hit and killed my mother, and then just left. They found her, though, and it came out in the trial that my mom had dropped her keys next to her car, and that delinquent pot-smoking girl never saw my mother until it was too late." Diane runs her fingers through her hair, feebly trying to put every strand back into place. "My mother died because the girl had lit up a joint and dropped it by mistake. Afraid it would burn a hole in her parents' car seat, she took her eyes off the road to find it. I lost my mother to prevent damage to a car seat." Diane shifts her back into the corner of the armchair and continues to stare blankly at the opposing wall. "I will never forget the sirens waking me up and how I stumbled to the window to see them cover my mom with a sheet. My neighbor took me out for ice cream after the funeral and before child services got there. I haven't stopped eating since. But you knew that just by looking at me, right?"

"Thank you for sharing, Laura and Diane. I know it was difficult to put yourselves back in that place." The room grows silent as they process the words that have been uttered. "Anna Marie, would you like to share?"

Anna Marie leans forward in her chair to get a better view of Diane. "Your mom sounds like she was very committed to you. I am so sorry she had to die the way she did. But at least you know she didn't suffer." She stifles a sob. "I worry every day that Lexi suffers, because she's trapped in her body and wants to speak but can't. I wish every day that I had been more committed to Lexi, like your mom was to you; that I had never taken my eyes off her. I wish that I had sat next to someone different that day, and had not been so focused on my neighbor complaining about her husband instead of watching my kids in the water. They were playing some stupid game to see who could stay underwater the longest. When I noticed, it had been too long. Too much time had passed before I recognized Lexi was under too long. Her brother had left her to play 'sharks and minnows', and she — well, she…" Anna Marie succumbs to the sadness and cries into her hands, heaving forward to hide her face. "I should have been paying more attention. When they put her in the ambulance, she was unresponsive. They finally revived her, but now she is in a coma. I screamed at my son, 'Why weren't you watching her?' I knew I was the one to blame, but I took it all out on him. He hasn't been the same since. I've apologized a million times, but I know he thinks I blame him." Anna Marie sits up, her face red and her eyes puffy. "I guess I suppose I do. I blame him, I blame me, I blame God, I blame my needy, whiney neighbor. I am so angry at myself. You know what the definition of insanity is, right? You know, doing the same thing over and over expecting a different result? Well, that's me." Anna Marie shakes her head, "I go over and over that day as though I can make it different in my mind. I even refuse to let my husband or son change anything that Lexi touched before she left us, right down to the sippy cup she used before going to the pool. It still sits on the edge of the counter. I just want to go back and make a different choice." Exhausted from remembering, Anna Marie buries her face again into her hands and sobs.

The group is overcome with a solemn sadness, and the air is thick with its weight. No one knows what to say. What do you say in situations like this? However, Dr. Abba keeps the session moving. "Kevin?"

"Choices," Kevin says. "They will screw you up if you make the wrong one. That's the truth. It's strange! You think you're doing the right thing and then, wham! You are in a place so dark that it's even hard to conceive that a God exists. I get it. How life can turn on a dime and leave you holding the bag when your intentions were only good from the start. I mean, I made my choice so I could help my family out, and look where I am now."

"What choice?" Jesse interjects.

"I signed up for a ROTC scholarship. I was pre-vet as an undergrad. That's where I met Kate. She was amazing. She would stay up all hours of the night to help me memorize my vocabulary for my anatomy class. I had been accepted at the most prestigious veterinary school in the northeast, but right before I graduated, my parents got divorced. Stayed together for the kids, I guess. Anyway, they couldn't afford to send me to school and hold down two separate households. Kate and I had gotten married, and I felt like school was now my responsibility; so I signed up for a ROTC scholarship. I thought it wasn't going to be a big deal. Join the military, get my degree, serve my time, and life would be great. Who would have thought that the next year we would go to war with Afghanistan? I had barely gotten into classes before they shipped me over there. My life's dream was to help animals, not hurt people, but I had no choice anymore. You do what you are told in the US Army."

"On my second tour over there, we found ourselves in an area suspected of hostile soldiers, so we switched to an offensive operation designed to develop the situation and establish contact." With a feigned sense authority, Kevin continues, "I was a US Army Soldier from 2nd Platoon, Bravo Company, 1st Battalion, 26th Infantry Regiment, 3rd Brigade Combat Team, 1st Infantry Division, and this got me face to face with a 12-year-old boy holding a semi-automatic in his hand and fear in his eyes. If I didn't shoot him, he was going to shoot me, so... I shot a 12-year-old boy. What kind of man does that make me? If I could do that to a kid, what kind of husband – father – would I be? I didn't deserve to have a life after I took his. I see his eyes every single time I close mine; so I don't sleep. The physicians want to keep me drugged up on anti-depressants and sleeping pills, but they just make it worse; so, I drink - a lot – and pray that when I do finally sleep that I won't see his eyes. I hate myself. I hate what I did. And I hate what it's done to my marriage. And school, the reason why I signed up in the first place, is now a joke. I can't remember what I read and I get headaches all the time from the bright lights in the classroom. But I'm too embarrassed to let Kate know so I just shut her out and I drink some more." Kevin hunches over his legs, his elbow resting on his thighs. His head hangs down, and his eyes focus on his laced-up boots.

Diane stands up and starts to clap her hands together. One by one, they join her until all are on their feet including Laura. Diane mouths the words, "Thank you" as Kevin looks up at them in amazement. Finally, they all take their seats again.

"Thank you, Kevin. I appreciate your service and your willingness to share. I know that you didn't really come here by your own volition." Jesse then focuses his attention on Christine and the last remaining story to be told.

Christine slouches in her chair, picking absently at her fingernails. Feeling Jesse's stare burrowing down on her, Christine glances in his direction. Feigning ignorance, Christine turns to look at Anna Marie sitting on the other side of her. Feeling Jesse's eyes still on her, she glances in his direction, his eyebrows raised. "Christine, do you have something you would like to share?"

Exasperated, she knows she must play along and share something that is actually the truth. "I wanted the turkey leg. I always got the turkey leg, but the year I turned five, things had been especially tough financially, for my family. My dad had to take a second job as a firefighter just so we could make ends meet. That year was also the year my aunt got divorced, so my mom invited her whole family for Thanksgiving. With more mouths at the table, my dad had to carve the legs, too. It was my turkey leg. I was five, and I always get the turkey leg. I told him I hated him, and I refused to eat dinner. I went into my room and slammed the door. After dinner, he knocked on my door, tried to make me feel better. He told me he'd buy me my own chicken the next day, that I could have both legs, but I was still so mad. I didn't want a chicken; I wanted the turkey leg just like every year. I refused to talk to him. That night, he got called out for a fire. He came into my room to tell me he loved me. I didn't say a word. He went to kiss me, and I covered my head." Christine stops, her eyes glistening. She folds her leg under her thigh. "I never saw my dad again. They said it was the worst fire our town had ever seen. The building burned for two days. I still can't bring myself to visit his grave, and I haven't celebrated Thanksgiving since. I just bury myself in work, even during the Christmas season, despite the pleas from my mother. I talk to him sometimes — you know, as if he's still here. But now he's the one that doesn't respond."

"You know, Christine, just because people leave, doesn't mean they stop communicating." Dr. Abba holds his pencil to his lips.

An unusual sensation overcomes Christine. "Ooooh." At first, she expects a rumbling of gas to escape from her lower regions. When nothing happens, she realizes that butterfly feeling in her tummy is the unborn baby moving around. "Oh, my God! It kicked me!" Christine blurts out as she grabs her slender belly in surprise.

Diane shifts forward in her seat. "You're pregnant! Now that is scary. If you can feel that baby kick, you have got to be almost four months pregnant. You're starving that baby!"

Christine blushes and looks down at her small paunch that is barely visible. "I don't have time to eat."

"You're a doctor, right?" Diane shifts her disbelief onto Laura. "Tell her she needs to feed that baby."

Shocked at the sudden turn of events, Laura glances knowingly at Christine and Dr. Abba but says nothing.

"Actually, she is my doctor."

Diane's disbelief flushes into anger. She shifts awkwardly to the front of her chair and points her plump finger in Laura's face. "What kind of doctor are you?"

"Hold on, Diane." Christine holds out her hands. "She's a wonderful doctor. I'm not keeping the baby."

"Well, even if you are giving it up for adoption, you still need to feed that baby." Diane slouches, releasing the unknown anger from her shoulders. "A baby needs food to grow."

"I appreciate your concern, but I don't want to talk about this anymore." A fluttering once again ripples across Christine's belly. "Oow," Christine looks down as she places her hands on her belly.

"Seems like your baby has a mind of its own," Diane smiles smugly and settles back down into her chair, folding her fingers and resting them on the bulge of her belly.

After the first semi-decent night's sleep in a long while, Dr. Jesse Abba strolls into his office, humming a soft tune under his breath.

"Good morning, Clara. How are you today?" Jesse hangs his heavy wool coat onto the rack by the door. "Sorry I'm a little late. I didn't want to leave the comfort of my warm bed this morning."

"No worries, Dr. Abba. I'm fine. Not too sure about your clients, though." Clara hands him the stack of phone messages.

"What do you mean?"

"Well, I don't know what happened in last night's session, but I have already gotten phone calls from most of them wanting to see you right way. Something about a dream or something." Clara shakes her head.

"Well, that is interesting." A corner of Jesse's mouth pulls up into a grin of surprise and curiosity. "Do I have any breaks in my schedule today?"

"Just from 3:00 until 4:30."

"Call them back and see if they can come in during that time please, Clara." He walks back to his office, balancing the file folders for the day, newly sharpened no.2 pencils, and freshly brewed coffee.

"Let me get this." Christine snatches the ticket from the waitress before she has the opportunity to place it in the middle of the table.

"Are you sure?" Joanne raises an eyebrow as Christine slides her chair out to stand up. "I thought we were going dutch like always."

"Well, I just want you to know how much I appreciate you being so supportive of me lately, covering for me at work and listening to my latest rant. Lunch is the least I could do for my best friend, right?"

"Well," Joanne grins, "I am pretty awesome. Thanks."

Christine places her purse on the table and plunges in to locate her wallet. As she pulls her wallet out of the overstuffed bag, a few pieces of paper flutter down and slide across the table toward Joanne. Christine's mouth opens in horror but finds herself speechless, watching the scene unfolding before her in slow motion. She reaches out to grab the escaping papers, but Joanne reaches them first. She snatches them up and turns the stack over to reveal the image of an unborn baby.

"I knew you were pregnant," Joanne shouts as she quickly flips through the stack. "I just knew it! You little liar!"

Christine slumps back down in her seat. "I'm sorry. I didn't want you to know, because I wasn't going to keep it." She focuses her attention on the small specks of bread crumbs scattered across the tabletop.

"What?" Joann's mouth opens.

"Why would I? Besides,what kind of mother would I be? ... I was told yesterday that I'm starving it."

"Who told you that? You know, all you have to eat extra for a baby is a banana and a piece of toast." Joanne reaches out to touch her arm as it rests on the table and rubs it gently.

"Really?"

"Listen. I know you. You're a control freak. I'm sure being pregnant is the scariest thing in the world for you; but I also know you are one of the kindest, most generous people I've ever met. You're going to be a wonderful mom. Maybe a little obsessive, but a wonderful mom, nonetheless." Joanne grins.

"You think so?" Christine questions Joanne, searching her face for confirmation.

"Yes, I do." Joanne exclaims. "You're going to be a mama!"

A glow emerges from under the surface of Christine's skin. Her eyes sparkle with joy, allowing the beauty of new life to consume her. "Plus, you know it is going to be magical for your mom. That's the best gift I ever gave mine. It changes your mother - you'll see. She'll do all this stuff for your kid that she would never do for you in a lifetime. It's hysterical to watch. Your child breaks a family heirloom, and she says, 'Oh, don't worry, sugar. We didn't need that Ming vase.' But if you had done that growing up, you would have gotten a lecture and an ass-whooping so bad you still wouldn't be able to sit down."

The excitement begins to fade from Christine's face, "I never thought about how my mom would respond. I guess I just thought she'd never find out."

"What do you mean? How would she *not* find out?"

"Like I said before, I wasn't planning on keeping it."

"Why wouldn't you keep it?"

"I don't know the first thing about a baby. Plus, I don't like feeling out of control. But then I heard the heartbeat, which was beautiful and confusing. I'm supposed to have an abortion on Friday." Christine darts her eyes at Joanne and then back to the table.

"No!" Joanne's body jerks back, rejecting the thought completely.

"I know, I know. But then I felt the baby kick me like it was trying to tell me something." Christine places her elbows sharply on the table and collapses her head into her hands. "And then to confuse things even more, I had a dream about my dad. And I've never dreamt about my dad. It was the *weirdest* dream. My dad was alive, and I was pregnant. He leaned down and kissed my belly, and then he spoke: 'Embrace the joy of this little human.' He said my anxiety and fear about this pregnancy was stealing all the joy, and then he said something about paradigms?" Christine furrows her brow and scratches her scalp, willing herself to remember his words exactly. "That we live in a dimension that has several paradigms, but most of us shift between only three of them. Then he described each paradigm for me: The First Paradigm – the illusion of time; Second Paradigm – a positive perception; Third Paradigm – a negative perception; and Fourth

Paradigm — a glimpse of heaven on earth. He called the fourth one the 'lost paradigm.' In my dream, he told me that this baby was the gateway for me to experience the fourth paradigm, to feel a kind of indescribable joy, but I was stuck in the negative perception of the experience. Then he started talking about Adam and Eve, how they lived in this fourth paradigm while in the Garden of Eden, the paradigm that is now lost to most of us. God walked among them, but when Eve ate the apple, it opened her mind to the other three paradigms, filling her mind with questions, fear, shame, and guilt. Because she did not know the gift of grace, she could not find her way back to the 'lost' paradigm, where love is all encompassing. My dad said this knowledge, this new way of thinking, created a separation between us and God. 'Find grace,' he said. 'Connect to the joy, and you will feel the presence of the Divine again.' Through this connection, everything else — the fear, the anxiety, the shame — would dissipate, giving me the opportunity to feel indescribable joy, the gateway to the lost paradigm." Christine searches Joanne's face for a response, for a sign of support. "And do you want to know the strangest part? When I woke up, it was exactly 12:12 a.m."

Joanne's large, stunned eyes stare back at Christine. "Wow... *That* was all way over my head. But you know what's *really* weird is if it was 12:12 a.m., you really dreamt it today, which means on 12/ 12/ 12 at 12:12, you had that dream."

Christine throws her hands in the air. "You are such a journalist! I'm telling you the secrets of life, and you are focused on gathering the facts."

"Secrets of life based on a dream — a message from your father? If you believe him, and it sounds like you do, you must admit that is eerie: 12/12/12 at 12:12? If that isn't a clear sign for you to have this baby, I don't know what is."

"I know."

She reaches out and hugs her. "You are going to have a baby!"

"I am." She beams. "I am going to have a baby." As those tiny but meaningful words slip from her lips, Christine's heart fills with joy, with the beautiful life growing inside her. Joanne said she would be a wonderful mom, and who can you trust if not your best friend? Everything will be fine. The smile starts to slip from her face, as a dark cloud forms in the back of her mind. How is she going to tell Johnny? What will he say? How can she work and care for a baby?

"You know, Joanne, I've just thought of something I need to take care of. I gotta go." She grabs her purse and heads for the door. "I'll call you," she yells over her shoulder.

Joanne shakes her head. "She keeps doing that," she whispers to the now empty chair in front of her.

Christine gets into an awaiting taxi, gives the driver her address, and then loses herself in the mundane scenery of the city. "Message received."

"Huh?" Christine jerks her head in the direction of the driver, who shakes his head.

"Message received." Realizing that the voice is issuing from her cell phone, she retrieves it from her purse and dials her voicemail. Two new messages.

"Hi, this is Clara from Dr. Abba's office. There will be an impromptu meeting from 3:00 until 4:30 today. Please give me a call if you have any questions; otherwise we hope to see you later today." Christine processes the information, then commands the cab to turn around and head in the opposite direction. She then presses the button for the next message. Johnny's voice causes the breath to catch in Christine's throat and her heart begins to race. She can tell that he was uncharacteristically drunk.

"Hey, Chris... uh... it's Johnny. Remember me? I remember you. I can't get you out of my head — or that night. Chris, I miss you. I miss..." His deep, slurred words immediately disappear, replaced by the robotic voice of Christine's inbox.

"What am I doing?" Christine mumbles under her breath. She closes her eyes and leans her head back, resting it on the seat and losing herself in her thoughts. "Maybe Dr. Abba's right. Maybe I do stop the joy in my life. I miss him."

Christine suddenly sits up, propelled by her revelation. "I love him! I've always loved him!"

"I'm sorry?" the driver uneasily glances into the rearview mirror.

"I love him!" She starts to laugh, a deep-bellied laugh that cannot be contained.

"Are you okay?" The driver's eyes dart from the rearview mirror to the road. He presses a little harder on the gas pedal, increasing the car's speed.

"If I'm having this baby, he's the only person in the entire world that I would trust enough to do this with."

Tears begin to stream down her face as she collapses back onto the seat. Christine can hear her dad's voice: "Embrace the joy." She can feel the lock on her heart open; all she has to do is open the door. But negative thoughts don't go so quietly, and their darkness begins to block the entrance, preventing her from opening it. "What if he doesn't love you in that way? We're just friends. If it was meant to happen, it would have happened years ago." Her smile fades from her face, stolen by fear. "I can't tell him," she mutters.

"I know it's none of my business, but it sounds like you really dig this guy." The driver glances back at her.

"What?" Christine wipes a tear from her eye with a gloved finger.

"It sounds like he makes you happy."

"Yeah?"

"Give it a chance."

"What? Him?"

"Joy." The driver turns briefly and looks into Christine's eyes.

"What did you say?" Christine leans forward, straining to catch the cabbie's words again, her brow furrowed in disbelief.

"I didn't say anything." The driver shakes his head. "I believe this is your stop."

Christine's face looks puzzled by the apparent auditory hallucination. She pushes it out of her mind as though she never heard it.

"Yes. Thank you." Christine hands him the cash while she opens the door to leave.

As she stands in the cold watching the taxi drive away in the snow, again her father's words come racing back to her like a warm ocean breeze: "Connect to the joy." Forcing out the dark, negative thoughts, Christine consciously narrows her thoughts to Johnny, and how much she loves him. Taking a deep breath, she presses redial.

"Hello?" The words barely escape Johnny's mouth before he hiccups.

"You're trashed."

"So what? You've changed."

"No, I haven't."

"Yes, you have." His voice is so soft and muffled that she can barely make out his words.

"Where are you?" Christine shifts from one foot to the other to calm her nerves and warm her body.

"I'm at a bar, trying to get you out of my head."

"What?" Doubt attempts to seep back into her thoughts, but she forces them back to the dark shadows.

"I said I'm at..."

Christine interjects, "Yes, I heard that. You've been thinking about me?"

"Yeah, so what?" Johnny grows quiet on the other end. In the silence, Christine hears a woman's voice: "It's your shot, Johnny."

Johnny clears his throat. "I got to go - I'm teaching Cindy how to play pool. A hot blonde with legs that go on for days."

"Come see me," Christine says then holds her breath.

"Nope, not going there again. If you suddenly want to see me so badly, you can come to me!"

"Okay." She starts searching for the train schedules on her hand-held as they continue to talk.

"What?" Johnny leans on his pool stick to keep him from falling over.

"I said 'okay.' I have to go to this group session, but then I'll take..." Christine draws the words out to allow the schedule to pull up completely, "... the Acelo Express into South Station. According to the schedule, I'll be there at 10:39 p.m."

"What?" Unable to comprehend the unexpected turn in the conversation, Johnny pinches the bridge of his nose, willing his brain to focus.

"Yes, I know this is a shock. But I need to see you." Christine looks down at her slightly bulging belly. "Actually, there's something I need to share with you."

"Well, tell me."

"In person. It needs to be in person."

"So you're really coming?" His wobbly brain is unable to process her words.

"Yes, at 10:39 tonight. Will you pick me up?"

"Uh... yeah...of course."

In the silence of a pause, Christine can hear the annoyed exasperations of the young hot blonde: "Are you going to take your turn or what?"

"Your little hottie sounds a bit cranky," Christine laughs, feeling more confident that they will be together soon.

"What group?"

"I'll tell you about it later. I'll be on the seven o'clock train out of Penn Station. Don't forget to meet me. Oh, and you might want to sober up a little before I get there." Christine glances once again at the bulge of baby and thinks better of it. "On second thought, you might need to have another beer to swallow what I have to say."

"What are you talking about?"

"Nothing," Christine says. "I'll explain when I get there. See you tonight? Oh, and it might be best if you leave your leggy friend at the pool hall."

"Are you seriously coming up?" Confused and halfway sober, Johnny rubs his forehead.

"I am. See you in eight hours."

"Settle down. Please, one at a time." Dr. Abba shuts the door behind him. The jabbering of excited voices echoes off the sparse walls. He is the last to arrive; even the unwilling Kevin has arrived early and is eagerly taking part in the discussion. Dr. Abba, unable to quiet them, is able to pick up bits and pieces of the animated conversation, that they all had a similar dream and, even more amazing, that they all woke at exactly 12:12.

"OKAY!" Dr. Abba raises his voice to be heard above the noise. Slowly the group quiets down and one after another, finds their seats. "Okay. Let's go over this one at a time. What happened?"

Unable to contain her experience, Anna Marie jumps in, uninhibited. "I saw Lexi and Brian, my children. They were both laughing and swinging on a pair of swings. Lexi whispered to Brian to tell me something. Lexi smiled at me as Brian turned to me and said, 'Mom, when you find forgiveness and grace, you will see me again.' I immediately woke up. It was 12:12."

"That's exactly what happened to me." Kevin shares, "I saw my wife, Kate. She was smiling and swinging on an old tire hanging from a big oak tree in a field. The sun was so bright shining through her short blonde hair. I could barely hear her whispering as she swung back and forth through the air, like an angel. She said the same thing as Anna Marie's kid. 'Find forgiveness and grace, and you will see me again.' Before I could say anything, I woke up, and it was 12:12."

Diane leans over her bulbous belly. "I saw my husband, Ben. He was so happy." Her eyes glisten over with unformed tears. "He told me that he loved me and all I had to do was to embrace the joy in life instead of just going through the motions. When I did, he would see me again. As he turned to walk away, I woke up and it was 12:12."

Laura sits relaxed in her chair, a smile affixed to her face. "I had a dream about me and Max playing on the beach, chasing a ball. The ball got away, so I chased it down the beach. When I finally caught up to the ball, Max was gone, but the words 'Find the Joy' had been written in the sand. I, too, woke up. It was 12:22, but I set my clock ten minutes fast so I'm not late."

"Mine was totally different."

Dr. Abba turns his head towards Christine. "How so?"

"I had a dream just like everyone else, but mine was about my father. He leaned down and kissed my stomach. I had to be close to popping, because my stomach was huge. The strange thing was that I didn't even mind it. It was so surreal. I have never seen him in a dream in 33 years. It made me realize how much I really miss him. Oh, and I woke up at 12:12, just like everyone else."

Confused, Diana turns to Dr. Abba. "Why did everyone see the person who was missing except Christine? Why didn't she see her mother?"

Knowing the true reason for this inconsistency, Dr. Abba looks at Christine and raises his eyebrows. "That's a good question, Christine. Why do you think that is?"

Christine's large green eyes stare back at Dr. Abba like a frightened cat. She knows that the time has come to confess. She glances around at everyone's face, all eager for an explanation. A horn honks somewhere on the streets below. Diane blows her nose a few times into a wadded-up tissue.

She takes a deep breath and braces for the blow. "Because my mom isn't missing."

"Oh, this is going to be good," Kevin rubs his hands together and leans forward in his seat, unwilling to miss whatever is about to unfold.

In disbelief, Anna Marie restrains herself from shouting, "You lied to us? We trusted you!"

Diane folds her arms over her chest, shaking her head. "What kind of person would do such a thing?"

"A reporter." Laura glares at Christine.

"Did you know about this, Laura?" Diane turns to Laura, on the verge of disgust.

"Not until now."

"Please, it's not what you think." Christine looks around, pleading for them to hear her out before the lynching cry. "I wasn't going to report anything about your personal stories. I just wanted to figure out a timeline or a common thread to the disappearances. But after everyone started sharing so deeply, I honestly stopped thinking about finding an angle. Lately, I've been more concerned about the baby; and after that dream, and hearing about your dreams, I'm even more convinced that I should keep it. If you let me stay, I promise I will not write anything personal. I will get approvals from all of you before I print anything. Please."

"Why should we trust you?" Anna Marie scowls.

"I really think when I tell you the rest of my dream, you'll understand. It could be very beneficial to getting down to the bottom of this, for all of us."

"Well, I'll say this," Diane points her finger towards Christine's belly. "At least your lying helped that little person inside you. He or she will have a chance now."

"I think we should make a decision together as to whether Christine can stay in the group or not." Dr. Abba looks around at the heads shaking in agreement.

Laura shrugs her shoulders. "I don't care, if it might help me find Max."

"As long as you start feeding that baby, I'll be okay with it." Diane gives Christine a warm smile.

Christine laughs, "I will, Diane."

"I don't know how I feel about it," Anna Marie says.

"I think it's pretty clever if you ask me," Kevin volunteers.

"Well, nobody asked you." Anna Marie snaps.

"Calm down, Anna Marie. We must *all* be in agreement," Dr. Abba responds.

"Fine," Anna Marie crosses her arms. "But I don't want a word written about my family. Do you understand?" she points her finger in Christine's direction.

Christine holds her hands in front of her as an act of submission. "I promise."

Dr. Abba turns to Christine. "Very well. You may stay, but only on the understanding that nothing will be published about this group, nor will any part of any member's story be shared. Are we in agreement?"

"Yes. Of course."

Laura whispers to Christine, "I guess that means you'll be canceling your appointment for Friday?"

"Yes, I'd like to cancel the procedure, but I would still like to come in and hear the baby's heart beat again, if that's ok?"

"I can do better than that, Ms. Becker," Dr. Laura says. "We can take a 3-D picture."

"Okay. Now all of that is resolved, let's bring our focus back to the dreams." Dr. Abba rolls his pencil between his fingers ready to capture any insights that might be gained. Everyone nods in agreement. "First, what do you think the dream meant? Kevin, any ideas?"

"I have no idea. It *is* weird, though. The more I hear about each person having the same dream... Everyone's smiling and happy, swinging in a field or at a beach. It makes me wonder if they're all dead."

"But if they're dead," Diane interjects, "why would they say we will see them again?"

"Because we're all going to die! You didn't expect this to have a happy ending did you?" Laura laughs.

"No, they're not dead," Christine says with a smile. "It goes even deeper than that. In my dream, my dad mentioned this thing called 'the lost paradigm,' a place that could be accessed only through indescribable joy. He explained that you needed to embrace grace *first* to remove the feelings of fear, anxiety, anger and guilt. Only then could you access the feelings of indescribable joy. I think the next thing we need to find out is if this is happening to everyone else. If people like us have also had a similar dream."

"You mean people like us," Anna Marie smirks. "Not like you. You don't have anyone missing."

"I understand this is hard for you, Anna Marie." Dr. Abba's smooth voice permeates the room. "We all agreed, and she is just trying to help – everyone – that includes you."

Unable to be swayed, Christine continues on. "I have a connection at the police department, and I'll see if I can get access to their files."

Diane's brow furrows into a question mark of doubt. "Isn't that illegal?"

Anna Marie shrugs discontentedly. "Why stop at lying? Why not steal information too."

In true form, the mostly-empty train pulls into South Station at exactly ten thirty-nine p.m.. A few people are milling about, waiting for the appropriate train to arrive and bring the anticipated passengers. Christine recognizes Johnny as he leans against the far wall. She runs her hands over her long brown hair to smooth it and adjusts her shirt. After a moment of thought, she buttons her long coat over her belly. The train station is probably not the best place to have this conversation. Ease into it.

"Hey, thanks for coming to pick me up." Christine awkwardly leans in to hug Johnny, wrapping one arm around his shoulder. "It's good to see you."

"Yeah," Johnny reaches up to pat her on the back. "It's good to see you, too."

Despite the screeching trains and muffled movements of travelers, the silence between them hums loudly in their ears, Johnny searching Christine's face and Christine darting her eyes from one place to another, neither is sure of themselves nor each other.

"Are you hungry?" Johnny's voice cracks as it breaks through the thick silence.

"I'm starved." Christine attempts a smile.

"Okay, let's get some takeout on the way to the apartment." Johnny slides his arm across her back and gently leads her to the door of the station.

Juggling bags of fried rice, egg rolls, and fortune cookies, Johnny opens the door to his untidy apartment and holds his arm out to usher Christine inside. The only light in the room is dispersed by a lamp in the corner, creating a homey feel throughout the space despite the clothes and papers tucked discretely in corners. A few picture frames are scattered around, filled with somewhat familiar faces from Christine's past: Johnny's mom and dad, grandparents. As Christine wanders around the room in the warm light, she notices more familiar faces smiling back at her: a much younger Johnny and Christine hugging and smiling for the camera. It had been taken after one of Johnny's football games, a game they had just won. Johnny's hair had been matted to his wet face, and his uniform covered in dirt and grass stains. Christine picks up the picture to look closely at her adolescent image and is startled to see joy on her younger face.

"It's hard to believe we used to look like that, huh?" Johnny places the assortment of boxes on the table and slides up behind her. Christine blocks his arms from wrapping around her waist and walks off staring at the picture.

"I know. It makes me feel so old." The corners of Christine's mouth turn down.

Johnny follows her and rubs her arm. "You really were beautiful."

"Gee, thanks. You sure know how to make a girl feel better." Christine feigns disgust, but his closeness unsettles her. She has forgotten how good it feels to be in his presence. She blushes at the memory it recalls.

"You're still beautiful." He grabs her, pulling her even closer. She feels a flutter, but it's not the baby. It's butterflies. She reaches out to replace the photo but misses. The picture teeters on the edge and then slips. Christine bends, her hands fumbling through the air in an effort to catch it, but her efforts are futile as the picture of youth crashes, shattering glass under the bookcase and sofa.

"I'm so sorry," Christine gasps as she tries to put the broken frame back together. "I'm such a klutz."

"It's just a picture frame. Don't cut yourself!" Johnny bends to help her, but in his haste, he doesn't realize Christine is straightening up with a handful of shards. Christine's head slams into Johnny's nose, sending a painful "thwack" to resound throughout the room.

"Oh, my gosh, Johnny. Are you okay?" Christine rubs the back of her head with one hand and reaches out for Johnny's arm with the other.

Johnny winces, bringing his hand to his nose and rubbing his wound. "Yeah, I'm fine. It sounded much worse than it was."

"Oh, my God, you're bleeding." Christine's eyes dart around the room looking for something to stop the flow. Feeling the blood seep through his fingers, he grabs a T-shirt on the end table as Christine runs to the kitchen, returning with an ice pack from the freezer.

Overwhelmed, Christine plops down onto the sofa. As he braces himself against the bookcase, shards of glass crunch under his feet.

"Maybe this was a bad idea."

"What are you talking about?" His voice sounds strained and nasally.

"Maybe I shouldn't have come." Her eyes are stinging, and she knows tears are coming. She tries to hide them, but they can't be controlled.

"Don't cry! I'm fine, really. It's okay. See?" He removes the ice to reveal his blood-clotted nose that is now puffy and red. Christine sees the collateral damage, and her sobs renew. She buries her face into her hands. Confused, and never good around a crying woman, Johnny kneels down in front of her.

"Hey. It's o.k. I promise. Are you okay?" He combs her hair behind her ear.

"Yes – No – I don't know." More tears erupt from the endless fountains behind her eyes.

"Talk to me." Johnny ducks his head to look into Christine's face, searching her eyes for some inkling of understanding.

Knowing she should tell him the truth, Christine opens her mouth to speak but finds that no words will come to her. "I'm... I'm..." She falters, "I... I just feel so bad about your nose; and I'm starved. It's been a really long day."

"I told you I'm fine. It will be back to normal by morning," Johnny says. "And we got food, right? So let's eat."

Her tears lessen, and her sobs have turned into little periodic hiccups. Johnny pats her on the thigh, then braces himself against it to stand. He walks to the kitchen and grabs the plates on the counter and the bags of take-out. As he sets them down on the table, he notices that Christine is still sitting on the sofa, wrapped in her coat.

"You want to come fix your plate? Let me get you coat. I'll hang it up." Walking back toward her, Johnny holds out his hand to receive it.

"I'm good. I have a chill."

"That's ridiculous. I'll just turn up the heat." Johnny holds out his hand again.

A glimmer of panic ripples across her face, but she unbuttons her coat and slips her arms out one at a time. She tries to give Johnny her coat, but his eyes are glued to the small but noticeably protruding growth of Christine's belly.

"Wow! I can't say that I saw that coming." He grabs the coat from her. "So tell me again why I couldn't bring the 'hottie' from the bar home?"

"It's not what you think." For the second time that day, Christine finds herself uttering those words. For so long she has covered up her life with little white lies and exaggerated truths. Now everything that comes to light is being misconstrued. "I can explain."

"No need to explain. It's none of my business. But it looks pretty clear from my point of view, unless of course it was an immaculate conception." Still holding her coat, he can't help but stare at her pregnant stomach. "I guess that answers why you haven't returned my phone calls."

"There isn't anyone else." Christine steps toward him. She can smell the remnants of the pool hall on his clothes, a nauseating combination of cigarette smoke and stale beer.

"It's yours," she whispers.

"What?" Unsure of her exact meaning, he looks her square in the eyes for an explanation.

"The baby - it's yours." Christine rests her arms around his neck. "I told you there wasn't anyone else."

"It's mine?"

Christine nods.

Confused by the whole situation, Johnny pushes Christine an arm's length away to glance once again at her belly.

"Shouldn't you be showing more?"

"I haven't really eaten much, because I've been so nauseous, plus I just decided to keep it ..." Christine freezes, knowing she has revealed more than she had planned.

Johnny removes her arms from around his neck, as he steps back.

"It? You were going to kill our baby?" He looks at her dumbfound at the very thought.

"I was scared. I don't know anything about babies," her eyes begin to water.

"And you didn't think I might want a say in this?"

"I knew you would want to keep it," she mumbles. "But, I wasn't sure."

Christine moves towards him and reaches for his hand. Johnny snatches it away, still trying to wrap his head around everything just thrown at him.

"Would you have ever told me, if you hadn't kept the baby?"

"I don't know!" Christine throws her hands in the air. "Is that really important now?"

"Yeah, actually it is."

Frustrated, Christine grabs her coat. "I can't do this!" and heads towards the door with tears streaming down her face.

"That's just perfect! Run away like you always do!"

"Oh, like you're the relationship expert. Remember, you're the one who's divorced!"

Christine opens the door and then, slams it behind her. Johnny starts to go after her but stops, knowing she will reject whatever he says. He goes to the window and watches for her to exit the building. Unable to get a cab due to the falling snow, she moves from side to side while rubbing her hands together. She turns and looks up at the window to Johnny's apartment. Their eyes meet and Johnny's anger dissipates as they exchange glances before she turns away. He rushes to the chair in front of the door and snatches his winter coat from behind it. He heads out the door and races to the stairway unable to wait for the elevator. When he arrives out of breath from descending the four flights of steps, he finds her entering a yellow cab.

"Wait," he gasps. "Stay. I'm sorry. Let's talk."

"I'm tired and I have to be back in the city early tomorrow morning"

"It's 12:30," he pleads. "It's not safe at the station this time of night."

"Then, I'll get a hotel."

The cab driver begins to get frustrated and finally says, "Lady are you going somewhere or not?" Johnny tells him no as Christine answers yes at the same time. The driver throws his hands in the air and starts to speak violently in another language. Johnny convinces Christine to stay and she steps back onto the curb. As the cab peels away, Johnny grabs Christine close, putting his arms around her to keep her warm. She pulls away and walks in front of him to the elevator. He catches up and pushes the button. They stand there awkwardly, both too afraid to speak. Finally, they step into the elevator as the doors ding open. Christine breaks the silence.

"You think it's so black and white about this baby, don't you? Did you ever stop and think you live in Boston, and I'm in NY with a job that requires a minimum of 70 hours a week!"

The elevator opens and Christine storms out. Johnny races to catch up to her and reopens the door to his apartment. Christine continues to rant as she paces.

"It's not your body that's nauseous daily and puking in your boss's trash can." Johnny winces at the thought, as Christine's grabs a handful of almonds on the end of the counter and starts crunching them with her teeth.

"It's not your career that's going to be halted by breast feeding and diapers!" Feeling overwhelmed and nauseous now, Christine walks to the couch and sinks down in it as she buries her head in her hands.

Johnny sees the fatigue written all over her face, and rushes to the kitchen to fix her some of the takeout food. He hands her the plate and encourages her to eat. Amazed at how quickly she scarfs down the food, Johnny comments that she must have been starving. Within minutes, she walks over to the table for seconds as Johnny's eyebrows raise, shocked by the sheer volume of lo mein disappearing before his eyes.

As she returns to the couch, she talks to him while munching on an egg roll. "Look at me! I've never eaten fried food in my life," she says, wiping the crumbs from her mouth. "You have no idea what I've gone through these last 12 weeks." She shakes her head as she takes another bite. "Just a couple of weeks ago, I was on a park bench devouring chocolate chip cookies and drinking milk from a carton."

Johnny smiles as he watches his obsessive-compulsive friend totally out of sorts. He walks over to her and puts his arm around her shoulder as she nestles toward him. Johnny looks straight into Christine's piercing gaze as she sits contemplating what he's thinking.

"Okay. Look. I'm not looking for some *When Harry Met Sally* moment. You have made it very clear that I'm just a *friend*. I use to accept that; but then that night at the hotel — it was like something I had never felt before. I wanted you in a way that I couldn't explain, and then it shifted into 'I never wanted to be apart from you'. Do you know I can tell you what you were wearing the very first time I saw you in second grade?"

Mesmerized by Johnny's words, Christine sits frozen on the couch, unsure of how to respond.

"You had your hair in braids down the back, and you were wearing an orange polo with white shorts."

"Oh, my God." Tears start to form in Christine's eyes again. "I can't believe you remember that shirt. I loved that shirt." She laughs as she sweeps the stray hairs from her face and smoothes them behind her ear.

"I know. You practically wore it every day. I remember my mom telling me on my first day of school that I couldn't have a peanut butter sandwich because there was a girl in my class that could die if she came in contact with peanuts. I remember I hated you until I saw you. I remember thinking 'She's really pretty'."

"Whatever," Christine laughs. "You're making this up!"

"No, I'm not. That's why I always ate lunch with you at your special table. I was going to make sure no one ever brought any peanuts around you ever."

Christine stares in disbelief at him.

"I liked you from the moment I saw you. I picked you, but you never picked me until that night at the Waldorf, when you whispered 'I need you. I've always needed you.' And I knew deep down inside that you felt the same way as I did. Then you ran, just like you always do."

"Why didn't you tell me?"

"Because I know you. You're too busy hating yourself for not being perfect to make room for love in your life. You always run, and chasing you never did any of your other boyfriends any good." He stands up and walks towards the window then turns back around to face her . "I love you! I've always loved you."

Silence fills the room. Christine sits frozen on the couch, overwhelmed with emotion as her heart's desire unfolds right before her eyes.

Johnny walks over to her and pulls her up from the couch. Christine stumbles into his arms. Brushing up against his nose, she makes him grimace.

"I'm sorry," she gasps while laughing nervously.

"I think I need to find my football helmet, if you're staying the night." They both laugh at the absurdity of their new-found awkwardness. Then, he holds her tightly in his arms and spins her around as he exclaims, "We're having a baby!" He stops. "I better not make the little guy dizzy." He gently plants Christine's feet to the floor, then leans down to rub her belly.

"Oh, so now it's a boy." Christine rolls her eyes.

"Of course it is." Johnny can't stop smiling as his hands rest on her belly. Christine is overcome with emotion again as she observes him, his face lit up with such joy. She wants to join him, to live there with him, but something is always holding her back. Doubt creeps from the corner, whispering to Christine that she will only get hurt in the end. After all, joy equals pain. Her body itches to run, but a quiet thought stops her. It lands on her brain like a weightless star, illuminating the dark and doubt. Without pain, there would *be* no joy. Inspired by the thought, Christine pulls Johnny closer and brushes her lips against his. Their bodies embrace, entwined into one. At that moment, Johnny feels the baby kick through the layers of fluid and flesh. "Oh, my God! I just felt him poke me! Do it again," he says.

"I can't make the baby kick. It already has a mind of its own."

"Well, maybe I can." He scoops Christine up in his arms and, like a bridegroom on his wedding night, carries her towards the bedroom. As he walks down the hall, he accidentally bangs her head on the door trim while turning to enter his bedroom. They both laugh as Christine rubs her head, telling him that she's the one who needs the helmet as they tumble down onto his half made queen size bed.

Johnny stares into her eyes and presses his body next to hers. "I've always been in love with you," he whispers in her ear. Christine, still tickled, continues to laugh until her giggles turn to snorts until she can barely breath. Ignoring her, he gently begins to remove her clothes while caressing her body in sacred places that make her laughter stop abruptly. Christine, hypnotized by his touch, lies motionless as time moves in slow motion, her body absorbing every second of every moment. Johnny wants to make love to her, to once again feel the connection they shared on that night at the hotel. A thought, however, comes crashing into his mind like a needle screeching across old-school vinyl. He stops. "We shouldn't do this. Not right now. I don't want to hurt the little guy."

"What?" Christine tries to refocus her thoughts into coherent words.

"You know... give the little guy a headache." Reinforcing his concern, he pounds his fist into the open palm of his hand.

"Oh. Stop! Can it really do that?"

"I don't know."

He lies next to her on the bed, pondering the thought, their bodies entangled as though they have been married for decades. The silence between them now is a comfortable one, content in the moment. Without prompting, Christine finds herself telling Johnny about everything. For so long, Christine refused to confide in anyone, so baring her soul as she lay naked on Johnny's bed feels freeing.

"You know all of those missing people? I think I may be on to something."

"What? I thought they caught the terrorists behind it all." Johnny drapes his strong arm over her and rests his hand on her belly.

"They're wrong." Christine turns to lie on her side so that she can face him. "I've been going to this therapy group where everyone has had someone vanish."

"Yeah, you mentioned that earlier."

"Well, everyone in the group had their missing loved one come to them in a dream, on the same day, at the same time. I think God is trying to tell us something. I think that's the key. I just don't know what it is."

"Did you have a dream?"

"Yes, about my father. He was telling me about these four paradigms…" Christine recounts the dream to Johnny, detail for detail.

"So you think this is some kind of spiritual awakening? That's why all of these people have disappeared?"

"You think I am crazy, don't you? This is real. This is why I am keeping the baby. This is why I am here now. I just need to know if others had a similar dream. I was hoping you could help me with that."

"Is that the real reason you are here?" He pulls away. "Because you need something from me?"

"Of course not." Christine grabs his hand and puts it on her belly. "We're a family now." Brushing off his fears, she continues going after her cause. "Your help would just make it a little easier. There are lives on the line. The president is going to kill those people, and they didn't do this."

Johnny leans over and kisses Christine softly. "I'll get you the list."

She smiles up at him. "I love you, you know." It feels good to say those words to him. She has lived without uttering those words, unwilling to frivolously throw them around like little pieces of confetti.

"I'm going to marry you."

"I know." Christine can't erase the happy glow on her face.

"But I think I want to wait until we get married to make love." He grabs the sheet and covers her naked body.

"Really? It didn't seem like that a moment ago." She taunts him and then rolls over to nestle into the nook of his arm.

"Yes, I want everything to be perfect for you."

"It is." Christine whispers. Unable to keep her eyes open any longer, she falls into a deep sleep as Johnny gazes at her belly with their baby snuggled safe inside. He kisses the cross, given to him by his grandmother, and whispers thank you to heaven as he closes his eyes.

Christine paces back and forth on the platform, in part from her anxiety and the cold seeping through her long wool coat. Christmas music plays over the loudspeaker, and for the first time in years she finds herself humming along. She glances at her watch for the third time in a minute; five more minutes.

To help pass the time, she digs in her bag for her cell and dials Joanne's memorized number.

"Hello?"

"Hey, Joanne. It's me."

"Christine, where are you? I thought you would be in the office by now."

"I know; I know. Something came up. I'm in Boston, waiting for the train. I had to convince Johnny to get me the list of names."

"Convince? Like the night you 'convinced' him at the Waldorf?"

"Oh, stop. It's not like that, and if you must know, I actually seduced him before I asked him for the list," she laughs. "By the way, I need you to help me make some calls tonight."

"Wait – go back to the naked part."

"Later. Oh, and one more thing. I think I might be engaged."

"What!"

"I gotta go. My train's here. See you tonight." Christine hangs up before Joanne can squeeze in a syllable of conjecture.

Upon opening the door, Christine comes face-to-face with an irritated Joanne. "I don't know how much more of this I can take." Joanne stomps into the living room.

Christine follows. "Hello to you, too."

"First you're having a nervous breakdown. Then you're pregnant. Now you're getting *married*! Not exactly in the right order, I might add, but still, all these changes?"

"I know. I know. I understand you're shocked. I am, too."

"So where's the ring?"

"Well, he didn't technically ask me, but we have an understanding, I guess. For all I know he'll probably change his mind when the shock wears off."

Joanne plops down on the sofa. "No, he won't. I've seen him look at you. I believe I mentioned that to you years ago? Can I hear you say it?"

"I know. I know."

"Say it."

"No." Christine covers her ears with her hands, knowing the words about to fly out of Joanne's mouth.

"I'm ALWAYS right!" Joanne boasts. "This is truly amazing — how your life has turned on a dime."

"I can't believe it, either, but enough about me; start dialing." Christine thrusts pages and pages of names across the coffee table in Joanne's direction. They scatter slightly, and Joanne quickly shuffles them back into a neat stack. "I have to focus on this story."

"Well, that's something new. What are we looking for?" Sarcasm drips from her voice like warm honey.

"Aren't you funny? We are finding out if any of the people left behind by a loved one had a dream, if they woke up at 12:12 a.m., and, more specifically, if they were given a message from the dream."

Joanne stretches her hands behind her head and leans back onto the sofa. "Did you catch the trial today? Those men are definitely going to be executed. Now you know no one is going to miss that! The entire world will be watching. A real live execution. The trial has been televised as if it was a reality show. What's the world coming to?"

"If they do, they are making a huge mistake. These disappearances aren't a terrorist act; this is a spiritual awaking."

"What? You can't be serious, Christine. You're not going to tell me you believe these people in that group."

"Of course I do. I had a dream, too, you know. And even you said it was weird that I had that dream on 12:12 at 12:12. Didn't you ever read *The Celestine Prophecy*? There are no coincidences."

"For God's sake, Christine, it was a fictional book. Your hormones are affecting your reasoning."

"Really? You don't think there's any connection between five people who have never met before, who have had someone go missing, and those same five people having a similar dream on the same night, awaking at the same time, and receiving the same message?"

"What I think is this group sounds more and more like a cult, and this doctor guy is brainwashing you and perhaps hypnotizing you to dream these things. I mean, before you started the group, you were having an abortion and hadn't been on a date in years. Now you're keeping the baby, which I think is a good choice, by the way, and you are getting married. I mean, you aren't exactly acting normal."

"You don't get it." Christine shoves the phone into Joanne's hand. "Just dial."

The White House has been extremely busy since Secretary Roberts spoke to the press back in September. Despite the chaos, the White House shines brilliantly with white Christmas lights, and every room is decorated with a beautiful blue spruce covered in ornaments.

In a small portion of the house, however, things have been much quieter. With Grace missing, the absence of patter of feet and echoing laughter make the halls seem more empty and the rooms colder. Tonight, the First Couple is taking the night off. No public addresses, no cabinet meetings, just man and wife sitting before a simple meal. If only it were that easy to lay everything else down.

The President places his aging hand on that of his wife. "I'm sorry we haven't had much private time together."

Caroline recoils her hand and folds them together in her lap. "It's just been so hard. I can't sleep. The thought of eating... I just want to crawl up in a ball, but I have the entire *world* watching my every move. I don't know how much more I can take." She collapses her head into her hands and tries to quiet her sobs.

He reaches to rub her arm and console her. "I am doing all that I can to get Gracie back. As soon as this trial is over, why don't we go to the camp? It might be good for us to get away for a little bit."

"It doesn't matter where we go. I am constantly reminded that she's not here, that she is out there somewhere, and only God knows what could be happening to her. And I'm starting to feel that your being the President of the United States doesn't help the cause."

"What are you saying?"

"I don't know, but if it wasn't for my dream the other night, I wouldn't have a single hope left."

"What dream?"

"I dreamt about Grace. She was in a beautiful place and was so happy. I have to believe that it's real."

"I dreamt about Grace, too."

"You did? Why didn't you tell me?"

"I didn't want to wake you. I remember thinking it was strange, though, because when I woke up, it was 12:12."

"I did, too. You weren't in bed, so I thought you were still working. I didn't want to bother you either."

"I was working late, but my eyes were so tired that they burned. I went to the couch to rest for a moment, and I must have fallen asleep. It was so real, Caroline. I could hear Gracie laughing. I was chasing her in a field, and then I caught her. I swung her around, and when we stopped, she said, 'Daddy, teach the world to love, and I promise you will see me again.'"

"Oh, my God." Caroline pulls her hand to her face, trying to process the words her husband has just spoken. "She said the same thing to me, only we were holding hands and walking around a lake. She told me to sit down on a bench, and she sat next to me. We were feeding the ducks, and she said, "Help Daddy teach the world to love", and I asked how. She said, 'Through grace, and then we can all be together again.' What does this mean?"

"I wish I knew, Caroline. I wish I knew."

"Holy crap, Christine! You're not going to believe this!" Joanne tosses the phone onto the coffee table and rubs the palms of her hands on her thighs. "I talked to eighty-five people and they all told me the same story."

"How's your cult theory working out for you now?" Christine glances slyly at Joanne out of the corner of her eye.

"This is too bizarre," Joanne scratches her head. "But you know you can't say anything to anyone yet. You need more proof, or you'll never work in this industry again."

"You know," - Christine sits next to Joanne on the sofa - "if you'd told me that a few months ago, even a few weeks ago, I would have said you're right. However, now, in light of everything that's happened, I don't care. Something in my gut tells me this is right, and I have to tell people the truth. Everything will work out. It's strange. But once you're at peace with it, the rest just unfolds."

"So who are you now? Yoda?"

"You'll see." Christine pats her lovingly on the knee. "Now let me get to work."

"Christine, you said you had some information you'd like to share with the group?" Dr. Abba sits in his usual seat in the circle, tapping his pencil lightly on his notebook. After last week's impromptu session, Kevin, Anna Marie, Diane and even Dr. Laura returned to their lives, asking everyone they knew if they had the same experience. Now they all eagerly sit around the circle, awaiting Christine's words.

"Actually, I do." Christine flashes the smile of someone who is bursting to tell an unbelievable secret. "I had a little help, but I was able to get a list of names, a list of people reported missing and the person who reported them missing. Again, with a little help, I called them all, and here's the amazing part." The group leans in. "Everyone had a similar dream; all one hundred and seventy six people that I called.

They all woke up at 12:12, just like us. They all mentioned grace, for-giveness, and embracing joy."

Diane gasps at the sheer number of people sharing in her expe-rience. Laura and Kevin slump in their chairs, knocked back by the strangeness of it all.

"Great," Anna Marie snaps. "But what does it mean?"

Eager to share, Christine continues: "I thought the same thing. What does it mean? So, I did some research. 'Grace' appears to have different translations in Hebrew, Greek, Arabic, and Sanskrit, but despite the translation, every sacred text points in the same direction: acknowledging that God's connection to the world as a whole, and to each of us in particular, is one of giving. When we open ourselves up to receive God's gift of grace, he has the opportunity to fill our hearts with joy; but we tend to stop the joy the minute we think it's too good to be true. We think 'Life needs to be hard' or 'This can't last forever.' The gift God wants to give us dissipates before we have a chance to feel the gift of indescribable joy. We were told in the dream to find grace and embrace joy. I don't know about any of you, but I believe that grace and joy exist now, and that we don't have to wait to receive it. I've expe-rienced more joy in the last six months of my life than the last twenty years." Christine's thoughts wander from the night in the hotel, to the taxi ride, to the other night at Johnny's. "Before I started to experience joy, my life was meaningless. I functioned on autopilot, going from one task to another. I didn't think so at the time, but after experienc-ing true joy, I now know my life was emotionally void of grace, hope and love." The rest of the group shifts in their chairs, attempting to comprehend the meaning behind Christine's words.

Christine takes a breath and continues. "Grace in Christianity implies a gift that God gives us freely. It differs from judgment, which is a punishment, and mercy, which is not getting what you deserve. It appears that grace is forgiveness, on all levels. You don't have to do anything to deserve it or receive it: meaning no matter what you have done in the past, you have been forgiven. And in Hindu and/or Bhakti literature, grace or 'kripa' is believed to be the ultimate key to spiritual self-realization." Christine settles back into her chair and looks around at the blank faces surrounding her. Only Dr. Abba seems to understand what she is saying.

"Thanks, Christine." Dr. Abba says. "So if we sit and embrace this new information, how can we incorporate it in your own personal healing?"

Diane, Anna Marie, Kevin, and Laura stare into opposite corners of the room, continuing to digest the meaning of what Christine has said.

"Okay, everybody, focus! Let's look at some different possibilities and see if any resonate with us. Let's consider the thought that there are always several interpretations of any event in our lives, especially in the hard lessons we go through. These events can ultimately empower us, help us grow in compassion, or devastate us to the point that we allow ourselves to become void of all love in our lives. Day after day, we unconsciously allow the event and/or person to continue to steal our joy, by not letting go of the past. It's our mind continually focusing on the situation that keeps the nightmare alive."

"That's exactly what my dad was saying in the dream," Christine blurts. "Our free will is the choice to choose how we filter the events in our lives. The key is to get past experiences to stop dictating our future, and to allow grace to give us a clean slate. He also said it was imperative to create a daily practice of gratitude, prayer or meditation to God. Because without this connection, the mind's sorrow, pain, regret, and fear will consume itself."

"Well, I'm glad that God was so willing to share all of this with you," Anna Marie retorts.

"I know you don't trust me." Christine locks eyes with Anna Marie. "But I'm only trying to help. I want you to get your son back."

"What is 'Grace' again?" Kevin looks quizzically at Dr. Abba. "And how did you get all of that from Kate swinging on a tire?" Kevin scratches the back of his head .

Dr. Abba replies, "You played Monopoly when you were a kid, right? Well, think of grace as a 'get out of jail free' card, the jail being all the thoughts that tell you you're not good enough, you don't deserve it, or you'll never be happy, loved, or successful again."

"Okay, so instead of living in regret and hating myself for what I did, I should ask God for grace." Kevin says.

"Exactly!" Dr. Abba nods. "But you don't have to ask for it. You just have to be open to receive it. That's free will. You can choose to be free from your guilt and sin and open the door; or you can suffer and keep the door shut. Opening the door is the gateway to a deeper connection to God."

"Precisely. There are many ways to access those doors," Christine adds. "But my father said grace and gratitude are the most effective."

"Well, that all sounds great in theory," Anna Marie throws up her hands in exasperation. "But what if you've tried everything you can think of? Prayed on your knees night after night? What if you're still hopeless, brokenhearted, and numb?" Anna Marie fights away tears. "How do you get from the hell you're experiencing to this Grace you speak of?"

Diane pats Anna Maria on her knee as Dr. Abba answers her question: "Everyone's story is different, and no one ever said it would be easy to shift your way of thinking after a tragedy has occurred. However, after you've taken the time to process what's happened and how you feel, focusing on regret, shame, anger or blame will only create an even darker personal hell, while the situation remains the same. Shifting to gratitude for the things that are still working in your life will help you move closer to the light and to joy. The key is to take it moment by moment without judging yourself if you slip up. In the beginning, you might have more dark thoughts than joyful ones, but if you stick with it, you can find the way out of your misery. There's always something to be grateful for."

"What do I have to be grateful for? My daughter's body is lying lifeless in a hospital bed. My nightmare still exists every day!"

"Yes, that's true. But did your son die that day? Did your husband leave you because he blamed you? Do you think you'd be where you are now if, along the way, you'd channeled some of that love back to them? Your journey would still be painful, but you might not be as far down as you are right now."

"I just can't let go of it being my fault." Anna Marie's mouth continues to open, but only uncontrollable sobs issue from it.

"God sees everyone through differently. But it seems we must first seek grace, which means forgiving ourselves. Then we can begin to focus on the things that are working in our lives, letting us experience the joy when it comes. It is those two things, grace and gratitude, that will help carry us through the dark, so we won't be consumed by the struggle or end up so heavily medicated that we're really not here anyway."

Anna Marie nods, understanding perfectly where Dr. Abba is coming from. She knows that is where she has been living the last fourteen months: drugged up on Xanax, estranged from her husband and son, and trapped in a world of "what if" and "if only."

Diane, unusually quiet, asks, "If grace is the anchor of our souls, how do we find it?"

Dr. Abba shifts in his chair to intercept Diane's gaze, "It's simple, really. Just start doing the things that bring you closer to God or the emotion of unconditional love. Try searching your life for choices that elicit the emotions of joy and happiness, the things that resonate with your spirit. Then keep your thoughts on those emotions, not on 'This will never last', or 'I can't be happy until this happens.' Just stay in the present moment, and when your thoughts return to all those negative things in your life that carry you back to your own personal hell, push 'stop' and rewind. Push the thoughts out of your mind. Then shift your focus back to God. You must continuously guard your thoughts because they are negativity's number-one target to keep you stuck in hell. However, if you start your day with God and continue to walk with him throughout the day, when negativity comes knocking, all entries to your mind will be locked."

Laura crosses her arms across her chest. "I never felt close to God. My Dad did, though. He bought me a dress and bonnet every Easter, and we would go to church together; but I don't do the church thing. I took yoga class once when a colleague suggested it for my hurt back. It was the only time I can remember when I actually started to master the whole thought-stopping technique, but it only lasted during the actual practice. It helped me become more peaceful by just connecting to my breath. Since my back got better, I've never taken the time to return. My schedule is just so busy. However, I did start using some of the breathing techniques in my practice."

Kevin volunteers, "I feel connected when I run, not on a treadmill in a gym, but outside with nature. I just haven't done that in some time, probably because I'm too hung over in the mornings." He laughs absently, but no one joins him.

The room grows quiet, so Diane speaks up: "I used to listen to a radio station when I was going through my masters program in Atlanta. If I remember correctly, I think it was called the Joy FM, believe it or not. Anyway, it amazed me how some of the songs spoke directly to me and it really helped me make it through the day. I loved that music. I have no idea if there's a station like that in New York, but I'd love to find out!"

Anna Marie wipes her eyes and blows her nose with a crumpled tissue. "I used to go to mass before the accident. I loved receiving communion and taking time in the morning to reflect. But I haven't set foot in a church since the accident. Sometimes I think about going back, but just can't. I'm just so angry at God."

"I used to meditate and pray each night on my roof top." Christine says. "I sat up there and talked to God as I gazed at the stars. If I saw a shooting star, I imagined it was God saying 'yes' to my prayers."

Kevin shrugs. "Well, I wouldn't hold on to that theory too tightly. In one hour, a person staring at the sky has an eighty-four percent chance of seeing a shooting star."

"Well I guess that explains why my life was always headed in the wrong direction," Christine laughs.

Diane raises her hand. "Okay. I understand the positive and negative paradigms, but what is this illusion of time that you talked about?"

Christine says, "You know how some people feel they never have enough time? They're always behind, always anxious about life because they feel that they can't catch up? How some people feel as though it's too late for them, they're too old, or they've missed their opportunity? Basically, it's people who let time dictate their life. Unfortunately, that one hits very close to home for me."

"I know what you mean." Laura picks distractedly at a string protruding from her sweater. "But what can you do?"

"In the dream, my dad said even Einstein believed time wasn't linear. If you feel that you don't have enough time, you'll be right. If you feel like there's all the time in the world, you'll be right. Time is impressionable. Ask a lover waiting for his or her soul mate to arrive on a train in five minutes; those minutes feel like hours. Chatting with an old friend over coffee for two hours can feel like minutes. So the long and short of it is that time is an illusion. Don't let it dictate your life."

"Got it." Diane nods.

"Okay. Let's incorporate what you've just learned and create a daily activity." Dr. Abba peers expectantly around the room.

"I guess I can try to go to church in the morning again. I just don't know if I will ever feel the same." Anna Marie shrugs her shoulders skeptically.

Dr. Abba smiles. "Just follow your heart. Once you do, you'll know whether or not you're doing the right thing."

"I've heard that before," Christine says, remembering when Dr. Abba used those same words on her. "I'll go up to my roof top each night and say an evening prayer." She looks at Kevin and then adds, "but I won't look to a shooting star for answers."

"I'll look into the different kinds on syndicated radio formats New York has available." Diane beams at the thought.

Laura squirms in her chair. "Well, I suppose I could join a yoga class again, or get a video I could do in my home at my leisure. I remember now — when I did take the class, people wanted to be all friendly and socialize. I just wanted to be left alone. I guess that's the reason why I stopped."

"Perhaps connecting with others might be a good thing for you," Dr. Abba offers. "Why don't you start with the yoga video at home, since that's more convenient? Create a daily practice, and then try to start connecting on a deeper level with your patients."

Laura reluctantly nods. "I'm not making any promises, but I'll try."

"Well, if I'm going to jog in the mornings, I guess I'll have to stop drinking."

"Awesome!" Dr. Abba shouts a little too enthusiastically. "Well, it sounds like we all have a plan."

"How do you know these changes will work?" Laura musters the courage to ask.

"I don't know," Dr. Abba says, "But whether or not it works, whatever the outcome, you will be better off."

"I don't care about being better off!" Laura rubs her hands together. "I just want Maxi back. He was my joy."

"And I believe you'll get your heart's desire," Dr. Abba remarks, "when you align your thoughts in a deeper awareness of grace."

———— • ————

Dr. Laura Windsor, despite her disbelief, has purchased a yoga tape for beginners and has managed to complete it a few times in the last week. Her heart wants to believe it really is that simple to get Max back, but her mind reestablishes doubt on a daily basis. After 30 minutes of yoga and meditation, Laura arrives at the office slightly eager for the day. She even notices the birds singing in the tree outside her office.

"Good morning, Sarah." Dr. Windsor enters the examination room to greet the first patient of the day. An eleven-year-old girl with black ringlets and large almond-shaped eyes is sitting on the table as she swings her legs back and forth. Her mom balances on the edge of the chair beside the examination table. "Ms. Thomas. How are you?"

Sarah's mom glances at Sarah. "Well, we seem to be having the same problem again. I thought that medicine you gave her would help, and she was doing better. But now she is saying that she hurts again."

"Okay, Sarah, I am going to take a look at you, just like I did last time. Is that okay?"

Sarah gives a shallow nod, glancing at her mother. The fear in her eyes as she looks at her mother sends chills down to the depths of Laura's spine. She brushes it off and gets back to business.

"You're right. It looks like another yeast infection, a pretty bad one." Laura glances over Sarah's chart. Sarah's big brown eyes plead to Laura . The old Laura would have ignored the fear in her eyes, would have said it was none of her business. Maybe the piece of her heart where Max lives has been made vulnerable in his absence, or perhaps Dr. Abba's words are finally breaking through. Whatever the reason, Laura knew she had to do something about it.

"I am going to write you another prescription. Mom, would you mind taking this and meeting with my assistant for a few minutes to cover some preventative action you can take at home? I would like to talk with Sarah for a few minutes, if that's okay."

"Well, I don't know," Sarah's mom glances at her daughter, her small body draped in an oversized gown. "Are you okay?"

Sarah nods.

"I'll be right outside." Sarah's mom slips through the door and into the hall, leaving Laura and Sarah alone in the room.

"Sarah, I am going to ask you a question, and I want you to be honest with me, okay? Remember, whatever you say to me, stays with me. Are you sexually active?"

Sarah turns her face to wall, refusing to answer.

"Or has someone touched you in places they shouldn't?"

The tears streaming down Sarah's face are enough to satisfy Laura. "You need to tell someone, or this is going to keep happening."

Sarah's lips curl and quiver. "I tell him to stop, but he won't," Sarah sobs.

Laura's mouth opens, and for a moment, she is twelve years old, pleading with her mother to believe her. Her voice softens to a sound she doesn't even recognize. "Who, honey?"

"Uncle Calvin," She turns her round wet face up to Laura. "He's really Mama's boyfriend, but it makes her feel better when I call him my uncle."

A sharp pain grabs hold of Laura's heart and squeezes tightly. Her mouth contorts to form a scowl. This is all too real, too close to home, as they say.

"Have you told your mom?"

"Yes, but she doesn't believe me," Sarah sobs.

The pain holding Laura's heart twists, flipping a dangerous switch in Laura's brain. At the risk of her sanity and her career, Laura steps to her surgical drawer and carefully removes a number eighteen surgical scalpel with a twelve mm chiseled blade, used in-office for making deep cuts. She looks at it, turning it slowly in her hand, and then walks back over to Sarah. She carefully wraps the scalpel and hands it to her. "Put this under your mattress. The next time he comes to your room, stab him between the legs. Your mom will believe you then."

***

Although it has only been a week since their last session, there is a noticeable difference among the members as the group trickles into the office. Diane looks stunning in a modern print dress and wears a satisfied smile across her face as she bounces through the door with headphones snug around her ears. The bags under Laura's eyes are noticeably smaller, and there's the hint of a smile in the corner of her lips, as if she has a secret that she wants to share. Christine glows, as most expectant mothers do, and Anna Marie's scowl is not as harsh. Kevin, however, displays the most drastic difference. His eyes shine clear and bright, unrestrained by the alcoholic fog that has previously clouded them. He smiles, not the sarcastic smile that he usually presents, but a smile of genuine happiness.

"Well, everyone is looking bright and chipper this evening," Dr. Abba observes as he sits down to fill the missing piece of the circle. "I can tell you all have been attempting to connect. How is that working? Kevin, let's start with you."

"I have been running most mornings, which means I haven't been drinking."

"I am so happy for you," Dr. Abba interjects, remembering his blissful night's sleep.

"I would say that I have had more energy, and I just feel better about myself," Kevin adds.

"I would say my meditations on the roof have given me a more positive outlook," Christine volunteers.

"What about you, Anna Marie?" Dr. Abba turns to face her.

"It's hard, but I trying." Anna Marie smiles faintly.

"I don't dread mornings anymore," Diane contributes. "I found an affiliate station that plays amazing music and I've even started to volunteer at one of their shelters. I feel like I have connected more with the children there than I did in the five years of teaching in the classroom. I return to work in a few more days, but the thing is, I'm not sure I want to."

"It sounds like your heart is really speaking to you, Diane." Dr. Abba leans forward, staring purposefully into Diane's eyes as if he has something life altering to relay. "Perhaps you should give it some thought. Laura? What about you?"

"My spirit feels renewed. I took your advice and made a special effort to involve myself more with my patients. The other day an eleven-year-old girl was in my office. I knew something wasn't right, so I got involved. She was being molested by her mom's live-in boyfriend, and her mom didn't believe her. Well, maybe it hit to close to home, but I had to help her, so I did." Laura's eyes fill with tears and she wipes them away abruptly.

"I gave her a scalpel to protect herself the next time that pedophile came into her room, and of course I called DFACS, but we all know how they can drag their feet," she looks towards Dr. Abba for confirmation.

Dr. Abba sits shaking his head; his mouth opens slightly in disbelief. "Not exactly what I was suggesting when I said that you should connect more with your patients."

"Maybe not, but it was very therapeutic for me."

Members of the group immediately interject with concern for the little girl, all speaking at once with no one being heard, except for Kevin's loud, deep voice. "While it may not have been the best plan of action, I agree with Laura's motives. Those government agencies are slow to act. At least that little girl has a chance of defending herself now."

"Perhaps, I can help expedite the process with DFACS, I have a connection there. Let's talk after the session, Laura," Dr. Abba says. "Now, let's get back to the original topic." They settle down into their chairs and wait for Dr. Abba to continue. "Did you find it easy to incorporate those moments into your day?"

They each throw side-glances at the others, unsure of how to respond. After a moment or two of silence, Christine finally speaks up, "Well, not every day. Life just gets in the way some days."
The others nod in agreement.

"That's true." Dr. Abba balances his left ankle on his right knee, fingers clasped in his lap. "Life has a way of doing that. Would you say that things went better for you when you took the time to connect at some point in the day?"

The members take a few moments to process the question, brows furrowed in recollection. As Dr. Abba observes the faces, they slowly begin to nod, confirming the positive impact those few moments of connecting with the Divine had on their day.

"You have all made great progress." Dr. Abba continues, "However, I want to encourage you to try to take the time every single day. Think of it as a supplement for your spirit just like the ones you take for your body. You don't skip those, if you want results so try not to miss your daily practice either. That connection, combined with grace, is the stepping stone to bringing back your loved ones."

"Hey, guess what? I miss you," Christine holds the phone to her ear, shocked by her openness. It has been so long since she allowed herself to be gaga over a guy that she doesn't recognize the sound of her voice or the words leaving her throat. Yet loving Johnny seems to be the most natural thing in the world.

"I miss you, too. That is kinda why I called." Johnny pauses, searching for the right words to break the news to Christine. "Don't be mad…"

"Why? What did you do?" Her heart lurches, bracing herself for her world to fall apart.

"I called your mother and told her that we would be coming for Christmas."

"You did *what*? You know I don't *do* holidays!" Her cheeks flush red.

"Hear me out… You know that your mom is getting older, and her heart can't take the excitement. How do you think she will take you showing up at the house with a baby she knows nothing about? She might drop dead from the shock."

"Johnny, don't be ridiculous."

"Okay, so maybe I'm exaggerating a little bit, but you're not going to be able to work through holidays anymore once the baby's born. It will be hard to find a babysitter on Christmas so that you can go to the office. Besides, it will be nice, visiting with your mother. We can watch *It's a Wonderful Life* in front of the fireplace, drink hot chocolate, and stare at the twinkling lights on the Christmas tree."

As Johnny continues to list off all the wonderful things they can do, Christine notices an unfamiliar feeling growing in her chest, a feeling she hasn't felt in so long that she has forgotten what it is… Excitement! Not just any excitement – the excitement a little girl has on Christmas Eve, waiting for Santa to come down the chimney with the present of her dreams.

———

Halfway across town, eleven-year-old Sarah lies in her bed with Theodore, her trusty companion. Her mother gave her the fluffy teddy bear on the day she was born, and Sarah has had it every day since. On the days that Sarah goes to school, Theodore waits patiently by the door for her return. On the days she doesn't, Theodore is her constant companion, drawing with chalk on the sidewalk; reading *Pinkalicious*; and dreaming of running far away to find a new family - a mom and dad that love her and don't hurt her with roaming hands and disbelief.

Tonight, Sarah snuggles tightly with Theodore, waiting for sleep to come and whisk her away to magical lands and mysterious people. Her eyes squint hard at the squeak of her door opening, praying that it's her mother coming to check on her.

"Sarah," a whisper bounces loudly against her ear drum, as she recognizes the raspy voice of her mom's new favorite friend, Calvin. If her mom only knew that he favored the younger, un-ripened fruit, but Sarah cannot count on her mother to save her.

Sarah's body cringes as he slips under the covers next to her. She winces under the weight of his hand as it tenderly strokes her hair. The stench of liquor and cigarette smoke singes the delicate hairs of her nose as he breathes heavily into her ear. Tears attempt to seep through her lashes and stream down her face as she prays to God to save her, to rescue her from this intruder. Calvin rolls onto his back and slowly unzips his pants. He then reaches for Sarah's little hand, still clutching her teddy bear with all the strength she can muster. Prying her fingers loose, Calvin places her soft delicate hand onto his growing member. Her body shudders with repulsion as she recoils her hand.

Through heavy breaths, Calvin whispers, "Do it! Make me feel good, and I'll buy you those purple shoes you wanted." Sarah knows exactly what he is talking about; she remembers begging her mother for those beautiful purple shoes for school, but Calvin refused to let her buy them. "I love you, Sarah. Your sweet, gentle face, your perfect little body…" He presses his lips to her face again and again.

Sarah twists her head in futile attempts to escape his undesired affections. His rancid breath envelopes her, and she can feel the bile in her stomach rise. As if whispered by the mouth of God, Sarah remembers the scalpel hidden beneath her mattress. She squirms to the edge of the mattress and, reaching down between the wall and the bed, carefully feels for the scalpel's handle she left slightly protruding from its hiding place. She slides the blade handle out, as he continues to rub his rough hands up and down her body. With the scalpel secured between her tiny fist, Sarah forces the words to come out, "Okay."

"There's a smart girl. I knew you wanted it." Calvin rolls to settle on his back, once again revealing his erected penis. With a quick prayer, Sarah, mustering all of her courage and might, swings the scalpel and stabs Calvin, piercing and pinning his right testicle to the mattress. As Sarah scrabbles over his thrashing body, an excruciating howl emerges from his lips. In her attempt to flee, his flailing hands grab her foot. Adrenaline and fear flood Sarah's body; she whips around and sinks her teeth into the hairy flesh of his arm. Calvin recoils under the pain, and Sarah dashes for the door. Swinging it open, she runs into her mother's arms.

"What the hell is going on?" Sarah's mother pries her loose to examine her daughter's hands covered in blood.

"He's been doing bad things again," Sarah cries, holding her bloody hands out to her.

"No!" Her mother shouts, pushing her away. Hearing the groans coming from Sarah's darkened room, she follows the sound. Sarah watches as her mother hesitantly makes her way to the doorway and then collapses to the floor, the sight too much to take. Calvin, managing to free himself from the mattress, lies groaning on the floor with a scalpel in his hand and blood streaming from his exposed genitals. Sarah runs to her mother's collapsed frame and wraps her arms around her neck.

Seeing Sarah in the doorway, Calvin points a bloody finger in her direction. "I am going to kill you, you little bitch!" He winces under the effort.

As Calvin's words reach her mother's ears, a strength rises up from a place locked away and hidden. An outpouring of love and sorrow rushes over her as she realizes the dreadful mistake she has made. How could she be so blind? Finding her feet, her mother scoops Sarah up and cradles her close. "You so much as touch her again, and I will kill you first!"

Sarah's mother slams the door shut and rushes to her bedroom, locking the door behind her. She places Sarah gently onto her bed, then scrambles to push the heavy dresser in front of the door for added security. As her mother grabs the phone to dial 911, Sarah hears heavy footsteps down the hall and an angry pounding on the door. Sarah's mother wraps her arms around her small frame while staring at the shaking door .

Although it has been years since Christine last saw her mom at Christmas, she still recognizes the same poinsettia wreath that has hung on the door since she was five. Despite almost thirty years of fading, it is still hanging on her mom's front door welcoming her home. Christine reaches out her hand to knock but hesitates. She turns to Johnny.

"What am I supposed to say?" Her hand unconsciously lowers to her belly.

Johnny rubs one hand across her shoulders and gently places the other on top of her hand resting on her belly. "Everything is going to be wonderful. She is going to be so excited to see you. Do you want me to do it?" Johnny removes her hand from Christine's belly and points to the door.

"No, I've got it." Christine takes a deep breath in and raps gently on the door.

They can hear movement coming from the other side of the door, and although she anticipates the door to open, Christine jumps slightly when it swings open to reveal her mother's fragile frame.

"Oh, my God! You're here! You're actually here!" Gail Becker is unable to contain her joy, throwing her arms around her prodigal daughter's neck. As they embrace, she notices the unexpected baby bump and staggers back. "What?"

"Surprise!" Johnny shouts. "It's so good to see you."

Speechless, Gail ushers them into the home Christine hasn't entered since the day she left for college. Christine and Johnny place their bags in the foyer and wander into the living room. Things haven't changed much, a few new knickknacks, but overall it is a time capsule of Christine's past. She plops onto the sofa, her feet tired of carrying the extra weight.

Slowly recovering from her shock, Gail remembers her role as hostess. "Can I get you anything to drink, Johnny?"

"No, thanks, I'm good." Johnny joins Christine on the sofa.

"Christine, let me get you some water. I bet you're hungry, too. I have some leftovers on the stove."

"I'm fine, Mom."

"Let me make you a cheese sandwich. That is all I wanted to eat when I was pregnant with you." Gail scoots into the kitchen, and Christine and Johnny can hear running water and banging cabinets.

"Really, Mom, I'm fine. This isn't necessary." Christine looks helplessly at Johnny, who is smiling contentedly.

Gail returns to the living room with a tray full of pimento cheese sandwiches and three glasses of water. She sets the tray down on the coffee table in front of Christine and then relaxes back into the armchair opposite her daughter. Gail enthusiastically slaps her hands onto her thighs.

"So... How far along are you? Is it a boy or girl? I didn't even know you two were dating." Gail pauses for a breath.

"Well, I'm roughly five months... not sure if it's a boy or a girl..."

"It's a boy," Johnny interjects.

"We don't know that for sure," Christine says. "It just all kind of happened."

Gail smiles knowingly, her eyes damp with the beginning of tears. "I'm so happy for you both."

After talking for several hours and enjoying a delicious honey baked ham, Johnny shifts to pull something out of his pocket as they relax in the blue sitting room just off the kitchen. "Well, I know it use to be a tradition in your family to open a gift on Christmas Eve, and I wanted to continue that." Johnny hands Christine a small box wrapped in red snowflake paper.

"What? Johnny, you shouldn't have!" As Johnny and her mother watch, Christine delicately removes the wrapping and carefully opens the box beneath. In the dim light of the living room, a perfect one-carat diamond glistens, rendering Christine speechless.

"Will you spend the rest of your life with me?" Johnny reaches for her hand as he drops to his knees, taking the ring from the box and sliding it onto Christine's finger. "I want you by my side forever."

Christine's eyes dart from the ring to Johnny's face and back again. Tears trickle from the corners of her eyes as she gently touches the clear stone. She opens her mouth to speak, but emotion lodges in her throat. With a gentle hand, Johnny brushes the tears away; Christine grabs his hand and nuzzles it, then leans in and kisses him tenderly. Nose to nose, Christine whispers, "Yes."

She would deny it if asked, but Christine has dreamt of this moment since she was five. She was home sick with a fever, and her mom had to stay home from work to take care of her. The family could barely afford the loss of a day's income, but they never let on how bad things really were. As she lay on the sofa, she could hear her mother's soft sobs as she stirred a pot of vegetable soup on the stove. Her father opened the front door and quickly placed his finger to his lips, signaling to Christine to keep his secret, to silently watch a surprise unfold. As he walked past her into the kitchen, she saw a beautiful bouquet of wild flowers, selected and picked by the calloused hand of her father. Her father reached out to her mama, revealing a simple token of love and appreciation. Her face, red with tears and steam, glowed brighter, and her lips turned up into a smile. He wrapped his arm around her waist and began to slowly sway to the music in his head. As Christine watched, her heart held on to that moment, knowing she was witnessing something special. She would spend the next 30 years longing for that moment, for a bouquet of weeds and a kitchen slow-dance; but this moment, this promise, are better than she could have ever imagined.

As the two embrace, Gail reaches for a tissue from the box on the end table and dabs it beneath her eyes, trying not to smear the remains of her mascara. Her heart sings like a church choir, overjoyed with her daughter's happiness, but she can hear the sharp sound of her husband's absence, the silence he has left.

Christine's face glistens with a joy that cannot be measured, but a cloud of dismay slowly shadows it. Christine's mouth opens in embarrassment. "Oh, Johnny, I didn't know... I've been so busy... I didn't get a gift for you."

Johnny's face softens as he slides a hand across her protruding belly. "You've already given me everything I could possibly want or need." Catching Gail smiling from ear to ear, Johnny shakes his finger playfully at her. "And don't think I forgot about you." He brings out another small box, this time wrapped in shimmering gold paper.

"Oh, you are too kind." Gail unwraps the box, revealing an exquisite gold locket.

"Oh, it is absolutely beautiful! Thank you! I have a feeling I'll have a very special photo to put into it soon." Gail winks at Christine. Johnny interrupts, "Oh, I almost forgot... The captain got a little something for the baby, too! He couldn't resist." Johnny rises from the sofa, slides over to his luggage in the foyer, and returns with a small bag stuffed with red and white tissue paper. Christine hesitantly removes the tissue paper, peeks inside the bag, and laughs.

"A Red Sox uniform?" Christine pulls a miniature version out of the bag. "What a surprise." She laughs again, holding the uniform up to her belly.

It has been so long since Gail has seen Christine, not to mention seeing Christine happy. It is simply too much for her to take in. Everything she had ever hoped for her daughter … Tears begin to stream down her face, but she tries to blink them away. Unable to contain her emotions any longer, Gail rises from her chair. "I think a celebration is in order. I'll get some sparkling cider." She sniffles and wipes her face with the crumpled tissue in her hand. She disappears into the dining room, where she gets her Lenox champagne flutes, and then heads into the kitchen for the sparkling cider. With tears still running down her face, she reaches for a new tissue to blow her nose.

"Mom?" Christine follows her into the kitchen; Johnny follows close behind. "Are you okay?"

"Yes, dear." Gail braces herself on the back of a kitchen chair. "I have just wanted to see you happy for so long now… it's just so wonderful."

"Oh, Mom." Christine wraps her arms around her mother.

"This is all too strange though." Her mother pulls away. "Just a few weeks ago, I had the strangest dream. Your father was cooking in the kitchen, and I heard this baby cry. The next thing I know, he's handing me this beautiful baby boy."

"I told you it's a boy," Johnny pipes in, smiling broadly.

"So, I'm just speechless," she continues. "I'm in awe just how good God is that he has brought you home with this amazing gift and that you are finally happy. I have prayed this prayer every day for over 30 years, and I'm just so touched. It's like my whole family is back together, and your dad is watching over us. He would be so happy for his little princess." Tears stream down her face again; her lips quiver, fighting back the sobs of joy. Christine reaches out to her mom and wraps her arms around her tightly.

The last two weeks have been an incredible change for Laura. She has connected with her patients more in the past ten days than she ever has in the twenty-odd years she has been practicing medicine.

Allowing herself to do more than just paperwork and examinations, Laura has joined a yoga class downtown and strolls through Central Park every evening to watch the sun set. As the days pass, she has grown to look forward to this new evening ritual. While it makes her feel connected to Max, it also connects her to something greater, to the gentle rotation of the earth, to the pull of the moon, to something larger than herself.

Tonight, the sun hovers low on the horizon, emitting a warm glow that cascades down through the bare tree limbs and falls on her face. Its rays warm Laura's skin as she meanders down the path on which she used to take Max for his daily romps. Her face lights up as a brief memory scampers across her brain. The memory is so real that she can hear his bark echoing in her ears.

"Oh, Max, how I miss you." Laura wipes a stray tear. She hears the bark again, a bark that sounds so comforting and familiar. She turns in the direction of the bark, seeing a few other pet lovers walking with their companions. She squints hard at a blur of brown on the path as it disappears behind a cluster of trees. The brown blur grows closer and gradually takes shape.

"Max?" Laura whispers. She takes a few steps forward, then breaks into a run. "Max!" she shouts. Max races towards her and jumps up to lick her face, his tail wagging uncontrollably.

"Max, where have you been? I've been so worried." She squats down, scratching Max behind his ears. As he continues to try and lick her face, Laura looks up into the darkening sky and whispers, "Thank you."

"Max came back!" Laura enters Dr. Abba's office with Max in tow.

The chatter of the group rises up, creating a loud hum within the walls of the small office. The miracle of Max's return fuels the belief that they are on the right path.

"You must be right, Christine. What we are doing – finding joy – it must be working." Laura beams at Christine, unable to remove her hands from Max's soft fur.

"This makes me want to work even harder," Diane confesses. "Maybe it will work for me, too."

"I think you are all on the right path," Dr. Abba interjects. "I know this is very exciting, but let's calm things down a little. Could everyone please take a seat?"

The room grows quiet as the group members settle down into their seats. Max sits on his haunches, alert to every sound from the street below.

"Max's return is a sign that we are on the right path. Unfortunately, he is unable to provide us with any insight." Dr. Abba continues, leaning forward in his seat with his hands poised in front of his face as if in prayer. "You have all done very well in creating a daily practice to help you make the time to connect, but I think it's time to take it a step further. Locate the places in your lives where you need to allow God to lead, this will allow you to release the fear stagnating your life and create a space for forgiveness to grow."

Little by little the group dissipates into individual treasure hunts of pain and darkness, searching for the proverbial x to bring their loved ones home.

Without bothering to knock, Christine barges into Hal's office. "You are going to love me, Hal. I've got an angle nobody else has."

"Ever heard of knocking?" Hal tosses the stack of papers in his hand onto the desk, then leans back in his chair, crossing his arms behind his head.

Christine quickly relays the happenings of the last few months, the group, and Max's safe return. "Perhaps this isn't a terrorist attack at all. Perhaps this is a spiritual awakening."

"What in the hell are you talking about?" Hal slams his fists down on the desktop.

"I know it sounds crazy, but what if these people have disappeared so we will learn to feel joy, embrace grace and learn to love ourselves and others."

"Shhh, shhh," Hal shakes his hand at Christine in an effort to silence her. He reaches for the remote, points it at the TV in the corner, and turns up the volume.

"We break away from your regularly scheduled programming for this special report. A federal grand jury of sixteen citizens has been selected. It has been a tedious process for prosecutors, considering the public nature of the case. Proceedings could start as early as tomorrow. Let's go live to Brad Givens on the streets of New York City.

"I hope the bastards hang!"a pedestrian exclaims.

Knowing the network will frown on foul language, Brad quickly turns to his left looking for someone else to interview as a young woman with dreadlocks exits a convenience store.

"What do you think about the trial?" Brad inquires.

"What trial?" the woman shakes her head.

"The trial for the terrorist who have been accused of kidnapping thousands of missing Americans?" Brad says a bit sarcastically.

"The only war I'm worried about is the one going on within me. Who am I to judge others?"

"See, Hal?" Christine interjects. "She gets it. She understands." But the other guy, he's too filled with rage and revenge, ignoring his own self hatred."

"What kind of spiritual crap have you been smoking? We report facts. Don't you *ever* come into my office with this kind of junk! The dog was lost, much like your mind these days."

Christine takes a step back in disbelief. Hal stares at her, examining her face and what she has become. She used to be his prize reporter, the hard-hitter never afraid to ask the tough questions to get the story, always perfectly dressed and physically fit. He shakes his head. Over the last few months, she has been nothing but a disappointment.

"If you want a reference for the *Enquirer*, I can arrange that."

"No, that's not necessary."

"Fine. Then get your head out of your ass and focus on the facts of this trial!" Hal belts out. "If you can't do it, Chris, perhaps you need to take time to rethink your priorities." Hal eyes her growing stomach repulsively.

"What about an editorial piece on Truths instead of facts," she retorts.

"I said No! Stick to the Facts or find another job." He then dismisses her with his hand.

With the coming of the New Year, the group has reaffirmed their personal commitments to connect with God, allowing Him to reveal his love in their daily lives. And as the storms of January pierce into February and March, the group experiences growth and change much like sprouting grass breaking through concrete. People around them are consumed with the highly publicized trial that is filled with fear and hatred, watching 24 hours a day, 7 days a week. Citizens continue to disappear despite the guilty party's current residence in an undisclosed high-security prison.

"Okay, guys." Dr. Abba takes a seat in his customary manner, balancing a notepad, a pencil, and a cup of coffee. "I hope everyone is finding moments of silence with God each morning." The group members nod, and Dr. Abba continues. "We last talked about finding ways to find peace with our past demons. How are we doing?"

"Well, I have stopped running and started eating. Can you tell, Diane?" Christine volunteers. "Now that I am eating for someone else, I'm trying to eat better — more vegetables and fruits and only organic. Oh, and I'm getting married," Christine blurts out, beaming and displaying her ring for all to see. The stone glistens as everyone collectively feels the excitement of Love being named, erupting in a spontaneous celebration through the clapping of hands. Quiet gradually returns as they eagerly wait for Christine to explain.

"Honestly, it was a while ago, right before Max came back. We were all so excited about Max; it didn't cross my mind to mention it."

"That's quite a momentous thing to not cross your mind," Diane exclaims.

"I know. I know."

"Joy is definitely a wonderful thing. I am so glad it found you." Dr. Abba leans forward staring briefly into Christine's eyes then turns and looks at Anna Marie.

"What about you, Anna Marie? How are you doing?"

For the first time since they all met, Anna Marie looks different, almost happy. It looks good on her. "I think I am making progress. I'm not there yet, but I think I am getting closer. I slept in our bed, which was a really big step. We haven't slept together in over a year if you know what I mean."

"And?" Dr. Abba scribbles a quick note onto the notepad.

"I felt connected. Safe. Loved. At first I wanted to cry, but I chose to just breath in the love between us as we hung on to each other. Then he made love to me just like he did when we were first married. It was if I were the only one he desired and loved in the whole entire world. He made me feel emotions in my spirit and feelings in my body that had been locked away for so very long. It was amazing," she breathes in deeply as though she's still intoxicated by it.

"I'd do anything to have a chance at that again," Kevin says quietly.

"Anna Marie, you have taken a huge step." Dr. Abba says.

"Kevin. What's going on with you?"

"I haven't had a drink in almost five weeks." Only Laura notices Dr. Abba's eyes gleam in celebration, having the nights of sound sleep that he hadn't had in over a year. "But I still have trouble sleeping sometimes. I just can't get that kid's eyes out of my head. Running seems to help me. So every morning, I get up and run through Central Park. And I've also joined a gym."

"I thought you looked buff." Christine jabs him gently in the ribs. "Your wife won't recognize you when she comes back."

"Laura, what about you?"

"Well, I'm taking your advice. I'm connecting more with others, not just the four-legged variety. And you wouldn't believe it, but I've even joined my receptionist for lunch. She's really a nice person."

"Excellent," Dr. Abba exclaims. "And you, Diane. Can I just say how great you look?" Everyone nods in agreement.

"Thanks." Diane blushes. While everyone continues to climb their own personal mountains, Diane has traveled the farthest this time. "I guess I just got a wild hair, as they say, and I started listening to christian music again and then I created my own playlist. The next day I took a walk to the end of the block as I listened to the music. The following night I walked to the end of my subdivision, and so on. And then I decided to join a gym and watch my calorie intake. I've lost over twenty-five pounds."

"Diane, we must celebrate," Laura exclaims, showing the most enthusiasm the group has seen emanate from her body. "We're going shopping!"

The warming sun begins to defrost the frozen ground of March to make room for April and the coming of spring. Despite the budding trees and the melting snow, neighbors, co-workers, and strangers can only focus on the fear of the disappearances. A self-proclaimed prophet named Elijah declares the coming of the apocalypse — the rapture has come and the chosen taken. Families sit around the dinner table, feeding on the negativity of the news and conjecture. The number now sits at 29,000 missing. Paranoia sits in every office building, waiting room, and parent's heart. Mothers shorten the lead on their children, home schooling them, anything to keep them safe. Government officials consider internment camps for practicing Muslims. Revenge feeds revenge, demanding justice and blood, as darkness spreads exponentially.

Another week, another session, and the group continues to progress despite the chaos around them. Dr. Abba glances around at the five faces looking back at him.

"I am impressed with the changes you all are experiencing. Why don't we share how your practice is affecting your lives?" Jesse makes eye contact with Christine. "Why don't you start us off?"

"Okay. Well, I've been spending more time with my mom. After Johnny and I visited her for Christmas, I remembered just how much I had missed her. We went shopping for a crib, and started designing my nursery over lunch. It was amazing, connecting with her again. I guess I've finally come to terms that in a lot of ways, I pushed away any possibility of a close relationship and buried myself in work."

"I know exactly how you feel," Laura interrupts, "and I don't want that life anymore, either. Max and I are actually going on vacation for the first time in my life. We rented a house on the shore, and we are going to run on the beach, just like in the dream. I haven't been this excited about something since…" She trails off, racking the dead files of her mind for a comparable memory, but resurfaces empty-handed. A sharp laugh escapes her lips at such a profound realization. "I guess work really did dictate my life."

"I know all too well how rituals can run your life, no matter what their meaning." Anna Marie's soft voice fills the silence. "I didn't go the hospital on Saturday, the first time since the accident." She lifts her head, anticipating judgment from her fellow members, but all she finds is love and support in their eyes. "It was such a beautiful day, you know, and Zack surprised me with a packed picnic lunch. We went for a drive up the Hudson River. For the first half hour, all I could feel was guilt for leaving Lexi all alone in that cold cement block of a room. I almost couldn't breathe; the air was so thick around me. So I rolled down the window and took a deep breath, asking God to help me find joy. And for a brief moment, I could feel something other than sadness." Her eyes mist over. "I had forgotten… I forgot everything somehow, including the simple joy of just leaning against Zack's chest on a blanket in the afternoon sun, enjoying a sandwich. Ham and Swiss cheese never tasted so good; so simple, so ordinary, but something that my soul desperately needed."

Silence swallows the room as everyone acknowledges the strength it has taken for Anna Marie to volunteer so much.

"What about you, Diane?" Jesse attempts to keep the group on track.

"Well, we all know how I hate change, or, for that matter, anything that disturbs my schedule." Diane laughs at her own stubbornness. "But I've actually enjoyed the changes that are happening in my life. The old ways brought me down, kept me stuck in my sadness by reminding me of my life with Ben. Now I look forward to going to the gym, and I just love the new Zumba class I joined. As of Sunday, I have lost two dress sizes." Diane stands and strikes a pose. Everyone claps and whistles at Diane's newfound waist and confidence. She returns to her seat with slightly redder cheeks. "Plus, I really look forward to volunteering at the Boys and Girls Club. It's so rewarding, giving back to kids who have so little."

"It's funny how everyone has gotten off a schedule and I have gotten on one," Kevin interjects. "I've actually made it to class on time every day for the last two weeks, and my first test grade of the semester was a ninety-two." The group breaks out into applause and whistles.

Once again, the group gathers on Thursday, and everyone has that uncanny sense of déjà vu. Smiles are a little broader; laughter and conversation are a little more fluid, and a pronounced bounce is present in every step.

"You all continue to amaze me." Dr. Abba settles into his seat, carefully cradling his cup of coffee so as not to spill the hot liquid. "You all seem to be so committed to connecting with God, taking care of yourselves, and being open to finding the joy in your lives. I must say, you have transformed much faster than any group I have worked with in the last twenty years." Everyone beams, patting each other on the shoulder. "What have you been up to this week?"

"I visited my father," Christine offers.

"Huh?" Kevin furrows his brow in confusion wondering if her father's death was made up also.

"In the cemetery," Christine clarifies. "It was the first time I've ever been. I talked to him a little bit, told him about the baby and Johnny." Christine absently rubs her belly. "I know it seems silly, but I told him that I miss him and that I am glad he comes to visit me in my dreams."

"I wish Lexi and Brian would come to me in my dreams again," Anna Marie blurts out and silence fills the room until Dr. Abba shifts the conversation.

"What about you, Diane?"

"I planted a tree for my mom. It's in my back yard, so I can see it every day and think about her. It's a Washington Hawthorne – my mom loved literature," Diane says.

"My life has definitely turned around," Kevin speaks softly to his lap, "but I still can't sleep. The guilt is so heavy, you know? It's like an iron weight has been put on my chest, and no matter what I do, I can't push it off. I can't run from it." Kevin shakes his head. "Every time I close my eyes, they're there, looking back at me. The eyes of that little boy, scared but unwavering," Kevin brings his hand to his forehead, shielding his eyes until he can compose himself.

"Perhaps," Dr. Abba softly proffers, "you should write a letter to the boy or his parents. Not to share with anyone, but just as a therapeutic exercise to release some of your pain."

Kevin nods his head. "I'm willing to try anything."

In an effort to lighten the mood, Dr Abba continues, "What about you, Laura?"

"I went on a date, my first *real* date." Laura cannot stop smiling.

"Oh, really? Who is he? What does he do?" Christine jumps in, eager for more details.

"Well, his name is Sam, and I met him on vacation. I was running on the beach with Max, and I didn't realize my shoe had come untied. He was running toward me, and right as we passed each other, I tripped on my shoe lace. We both toppled over to the ground. I was so embarrassed, I didn't know what to say. He was so attractive, my tongue wouldn't work. Max loved him immediately, and he just fell all over Max, scratching him behind the ears and everything. Well, to make a long story short, he asked me for coffee. I accepted." Laura's cheeks glow red with a child's infatuation. "We sat for three hours, talking about anything and everything. Then he walked me back to my rental house."

"Did he kiss you goodnight?" Diane interrupts.

"No, even better. He hugged me. It felt so nice in his strong embrace." Laura giggles.

"Oh, brother." Kevin rolls his eyes at all of the estrogen in the room. He looks for manly support from Dr. Abba, but he should know better. Dr. Abba has a goofy grin on his face, overcome with excitement for his former colleague and friend finally opening her heart.

The brisk winds of winter have grown tired and warm, stalling with the thunderous rains of spring. The blooming buds release their scent, providing an appealing aroma for the beautiful birth of spring.

Saturday morning starts with a glistening of dew on the lime-green blades of grass pushing through the sidewalk cracks that lead Diane to the center of hopelessness. She looks down at the piece of paper, then slowly enters the stairwell to climb the two flights of stairs. Not knowing what to say when the door opens, Diane takes a deep breath and whispers a small prayer for God to give her the right words at the right time. A dog barks somewhere below, and a baby's cries seep through the apartment next door. A gruff man shouts down the stairwell from a flight up, and Diane's heart begins to beat faster as she looks around at the filth scattered along the stairwell. She raises her shaking hand to knock.

"Who is it?" a scratchy voice shouts.

With slightly more nerve, Diane knocks again.

"All right already. I'm coming."

Diane can hear muffled movements then notices the doorknob start to turn. The sunken face on the other side had left the chain on the latch, unsure of the unexpected visitor. Diane smiles at her.

"I don't have any money." The woman steps back to shut the door.

"I don't want any money." Diane interjects, sliding her foot towards the door. "Are you Tonya?"

"Why? Who wants to know?"

"If you are, I have a present for you."

"Hold on a second." She shuts the door to remove the latch, then reopens the door a little wider. The stench of stale marijuana drifts from the apartment. Diane fights the urge to cough.

"I'm Tonya." She folds her arms across her chest, revealing a few faded tattoos and a nasty bruise on her right arm.

"Twenty years ago today you hit my mother with your car and killed her."

"What? I don't have to listen to this. Get out of here." She steps back to close the door, but it finds the forceful end of Diane's foot instead.

"I came to tell you I forgive you. I hated you. You stole my mother, the only person in my life, and you took her from me. They put me in foster care. Did you know that?"

Tonya wipes her eyes to avoid the forming tears from escaping. She remains quiet, unable to look at Diane.

"God must have great things in store for you," Diane says.

The tears now flow freely down Tonya's face. Diane pulls Tonya to her, wrapping her thick arms around her frail frame. Tonya's body collapses, her full weight leaning on Diane and heaving with the release of every sob.

"I am so sorry..."

"I forgive you," Diane whispers into her ear. "But make it count. Make something of your life."

Tonya straightens slightly, pulling away to look into Diane's eyes.

"God doesn't make mistakes, Tonya." Diane smiles through her own tears. "He saved you. Make it count."

Diane reaches into her purse and pulls out a pen and scratch paper. She scribbles her number and then thrusts it into Tonya's hand. "Here is my contact information. Let me know if I can do anything to help you. I know some people who might be able to help you straighten out your life." Diane turns to head down the stairs. "Goodbye, Tonya."

Tonya remains in the doorway as Diane disappears beneath the stairwell.

Diane finds her way down the remaining flight of stairs and blindingly steps into the sunlight and fresh air. As her eyes adjust, a figure appears in front of her. She blinks again.

"Oh, my God," Diane shouts as she runs into the arms of her husband.

"I thought I would never see you again."

Ben pulls Diane to him and hugs her tightly, so tight, Diane can feel her lungs struggle slightly to replenish with air.

"I thought you left me," Diane gasps.

"I would never leave you, " Ben smiles at her, admiring his wife's painted face and fitter frame.

"What happened? Where did you go?" Ben takes Diane by the hand, intertwining his fingers with hers. "Let's take a walk." They head back towards the center of town, enjoying the renewal of spring.

"It was the strangest thing, Dee. I woke up in the morning and looked around. It was like I was stuck in that movie where you wake up and it's the same day. That's how I felt, in our life, reliving the same day, every day. I didn't have any joy, I didn't have expectations, I was totally indifferent. I looked in the mirror at what I had become, and my eyes puddled with tears. I couldn't see through them, and as

I searched for my reflection in the mirror, I somehow went through to the other side, just like Alice in Wonderland, but it was a different perception of our life. Another paradigm, another possibility. We were together in a different house, and I was getting ready to take our boys out to..."

"We had children?" Diane interrupts, overcome with the thought of having children.

"Yes," Ben exclaims. "And we were both healthy, fit and active; and we had sex all the time." He winks at her, and pulls Diane against the front of his body. She blushes at his directness.

"And we were happy, Dee. You still organized everything, but you were much more laid back. You trusted life more. You turned the loss of your mother into a mission to help orphaned children. Our twin boys lost their parents in a car crash when they were five months old."

Diane wipes the tears flooding from her eyes. Every wish she has ever had is flowing from her husband's mouth. It was almost too much to take.

"Oh, Ben, it sounds too good to be true."

"No, it's not, and that's the kind of thinking that's been keeping us stuck in the prison of monotony. Life is not supposed to be hard, but somehow we have come to believe collectively that it is, and so life is hard. In this other paradigm Diane, you didn't allow fear and sadness to rule your life. You lived faithfully in the present." Ben smiles. "I've been watching you, and you are doing it: feeling the presence of God in your life, experiencing joy, facing your addictions, working out, eating healthy, volunteering, and now this..." He points over his shoulder at the projects fading into the distance. "The way you are thinking and acting now is closer to the dimension in which I've been living."

Diane grabs Ben's arm and rests her head on his shoulder as they continue to walk through the streets of downtown, his deep voice relaying everything he has learned over the past months.

As soon as Diane and Ben return home, she immediately calls Dr. Abba with the news and requests an impromptu session. When everyone hears the news, all eagerly await for Diane and Ben to arrive and pounce on them when they do.

"Settle down, settle down." Dr. Abba raises and lowers his hands in an effort to quiet down the excited group.

"When did this happen? How did it occur?" Everyone talks at once, each question asked louder than the last. Dr. Abba once again repeats his request. "Settle down!" Their voices lower into silence as they find their seats.

"Diane, please tell us everything." Dr. Abba leans back into his seat, laughing silently at their eagerness.

"I had gone to talk to Tonya, to let her know that I forgave her, and there he was, standing in the light. I had let go of the hatred and pain of losing my mother and embraced forgiveness, just like we talked about." Diane clings to Ben's arm, afraid to let go and find that it is all a dream.

"Okay," Laura mutters, thinking aloud. "We know we are on the right track, but how do we get the word out? How do we let people know this is a spiritual phenomenon, not a terrorist attack?"

"Why don't you call Oprah? She's into all this spiritual stuff, right?" Kevin comments.

Diane replies, "That's not such a bad idea. You know the news stations won't have anything to do with this."

"Don't be ridiculous." Laura flips her hand carelessly to the side. "Oprah is over, off the air."

"Not really, I wouldn't say owning your *own* network exactly over." Diane places her finger to her lips thoughtfully.

"Well, even so, it would be impossible to get to Oprah personally, and her staff members would think we were all lunatics," Laura continues.

" Oprah might even think we're crazy, but we have to try," Diane pleads.

"Maybe I can help," Christine responds, picking up her cell phone. "My old college roommate worked for her last time we talked." She waits for her friend's voice, her leg jittering with anticipation. "Carol? Hi, it's me, Christine. Yes, I know it's been awhile. Hey, listen. I need a favor. Do you still work for Oprah? Wonderful! What? I don't believe it. You are sitting with Gayle King right now? Could I speak to her for a minute? It's about the president's daughter."

Diane's mouth drops. "If that isn't the orchestration of God, I don't know what is."

"That's pretty freaky," Kevin agrees.

"Not freaky. Divine," Dr. Abba whispers.

———

"Thank you all for joining us for tonight's special." Oprah sits comfortably on her old set, revived for this special broadcast on OWN. "We have on-stage tonight a missing person now found. Diane Couch claims that her husband, Ben, disappeared back in September, along with thousands of others, but a week ago, he returned with an interesting message." Oprah turns to Ben and Diane. "Ben, tell us a little about your story."

"Well, it's a little hard to explain, so bear with me. When I disappeared, it was like living in an alternate reality. In this alternate reality, both Diane and I had made different choices." Ben lovingly pats his wife on the knee. Diane slides her arm through the crook of his to help calm her nerves.

"What do you mean by 'different choices'?" Oprah prods Ben to continue.

"After her mother died, life was hard for Diane. She shut herself off and looked to food and routine for comfort. In this alternate reality, she still became a teacher, but she wrote a grant and developed a program for orphaned children. She was much healthier; about 30 pounds lighter; and after we were married, we fostered twin boys who had lost their parents in an automobile accident. From where I was, I could see between the worlds, see the different choices and the different emotions that ruled our lives. I could feel the void in our souls in one reality and the love and joy in the other reality simultaneously. In this alternate paradigm, instead of sitting at home and watching TV every night, Diane worked with her children's program, and I coached our sons' T-ball team. On the weekend, we all ran around having wonderful adventures together."

"Diane, what were you thinking when Ben didn't come home?" Oprah turns to Diane.

"I thought he had left me. Neither of us had been *living* for quite some time, and I just thought he was fed up. Then I joined a therapy group for the missing because if I didn't I might have been laid off."

"We have the group members here with us today." Oprah extends her arm in the direction of the front row as the camera takes a panorama shot, capturing them all on film. "And Diane, it was after you joined this group that something unusual happened to you, to all of you, right?"

"That's right. I had a dream, just like every other member of the group, on December 12, 2012. In my dream, Ben came to me and told me to seek grace, and I would see him again. It was actually Christine who pieced it all together."

"Christine, tell us what happened." Oprah motions to the stage hand to pass her the microphone.

"My father explained it perfectly to me. I hope that I can do it justice so that you can understand its importance. Whatever message you received, that is the key to each person's personal healing. Some people need to learn to love and forgive themselves; some need to give up their addictions; and some may need to forgive someone else, and learn to open their hearts and live again. Others may need to break away from the chains of time and negative thoughts, creating a no-win reality day after day. However, the very first step for all of us is to find God's grace and presence through a daily ritual, something that appears to be very simple but is challenging to commit to each day. The next step is to focus on what is working in our lives, and to be open to receive joy regardless of what we are going through. The final step is to stay open while we receive God's joy, to not run away or think negative thoughts like 'this can't be real' or 'this will never last.' Once you master this, as Diane has done, it seems to trigger the return of your loved one."

"Hey, Hal. I should be in the office in an hour." Christine braces her cell phone delicately on her shoulder and runs a comb through her wet hair.

"Don't bother coming in."

"What? What are you talking about?" Christine lays the comb down on the counter and stares at her unmade face in the mirror. Drops of water drip down from the tips of her hair and run down her bare shoulders.

"I talked with Simon a few minutes ago. It appears that his girl-friend saw you last night."

"Oh, really? Where?" Christine feigns ignorance.

"Don't play stupid, Christine. You know exactly where she saw you. You didn't think you could go on national television spouting that crap and not think anyone would notice."

"I'm sorry, Hal. You wouldn't listen. I had to get the word out. People should know," Christine says.

"You're fired."

Before Christine can respond, ask for a second chance, Hal hangs up the phone, leaving Christine with a large hole in the bottom of her stomach.

"Bizarre happenings for tonight's report," Brad recites from the teleprompter. "People are going out of their way to be nice to one another, and random acts of kindness are being reported all over the country following last night's impromptu broadcast by the Oprah Winfrey Network. It is believed that these random acts of kindness will bring the missing thousands home to their loved ones. But half the nation stands firmly in the belief that this is an act of hate and Oprah's show has yet to be validated."

"We, the jury, find the defendant guilty of all charges. We hereby sentence the defendant to death by lethal injection as ordered by the President of the United States."

Cheers erupt from the courtroom, and rioters invade the streets of D.C., celebrating the win for America. The convicted regime leader is whisked away to a stuffy grey interrogation room, absent of windows. Fluorescent lights flicker down onto the President of the United States, sitting in the opposite chair; his legs are crossed, and a scowl stretches across his thin lips.

"I've been waiting for you. Please have a seat."

The prisoner sits across from the president, his handcuffed hands resting in his lap. Silence rings in their ears, but then the President opens his mouth to speak.

"Tell me where my daughter is, and I will spare your life," he whispers.

"I would tell you if I knew. My son – has also vanished."

"You expect me to believe that?" The president removes a tattered note from his breast pocket. "'Your daughter is an infidel to be executed like the others.' Those are your words, and you expect me to believe that you don't know where she is, that you would *tell* me if you did?" He slams his fists down onto to tabletop, the sound of his force echoing through the cement room.

"Please, I don't know where she is," the man pleads.

Blood rushes to the president's face, and his anger rises. He grits his teeth, willing his mind to overcome the urge to strike him. He is desperate, knowing that if he comes up empty-handed, Gracie will be lost to him forever. He towers over the convicted terrorist. *"For the last time, tell me where she is."*

"I don't know." The scruffy man's eyes bulge with fear.

Unable to contain his anger any longer, the President releases a hard mist of spit across the regime leader's face. He turns to the guarding soldier. "You have 3 days to get him to speak. If he doesn't tell me where my daughter is, I will kill him myself."

———————

Anna Marie sits on the pew alone, close to the back where she won't be noticed. She shifts in her seat and glances around. The stained-glass windows, columns, and buttresses are all so familiar to her. So much of her life happened here: Brian's and Lexi's baptisms, her wedding, her father's funeral. The sanctuary was a place in which she felt at home, but now she feels like an unwanted guest. Her eyes water as a familiar hymn resounds through the vaulted ceiling and surrounds her. She kneels against the pew in front of her and buries her face in her hands, quietly weeping.

"Heavenly Father, help me to stay," Anna Marie whispers into her palms.

"Even Jesus had doubt when He cried out, 'My God, my God, why have you forsaken me.'" The priest's booming voice resonates throughout the sanctuary. Anna Marie lifts her head, wiping tears away from her cheeks. "All of us go through dark times, and it is then that we need God most, that we tend to question his existence. Most people think faith comes from answered prayers. I find it is more accurate to say that it is our brokenness that brings us to God, this is exactly the opposite of what most believe. It can take a lifetime, even with grace, to accept such a paradox. Grace creates the very emptiness that grace alone can fill."

The priest's words stir a deep place at the core of Anna Marie's soul, and tears once again flow freely. "But I can't find the grace," Anna Marie whispers to herself.

A woman, also sitting alone on the pew in front of Anna Marie, digs in her purse for a tissue. "Here," she whispers, thrusting the tissue in her direction.

"Thank you." Anna Marie reaches to accept it, and in doing so, notices the replica of the pieta as if seeing it for the first time. As if placed there by God, a thought runs through her mind. How could Mary endure holding the crucified body of her son? As that thought vanishes, another replaces it: *because she didn't do it alone.*

"I have been doing everything alone and failing miserably," she thinks. As she looks up at the Pieta, Anna Marie whispers, "Help me find forgiveness. Jesus, come back into my heart."

A warmth envelopes her, followed by a feeling of peace. She smiles, her eyes closed, and suddenly she feels a light hand on her shoulder. She turns to find the image of her son, Brian.

"Oh, my God! Brian!" In one swift motion, Anna Marie grabs her son into her arms. "Thank you, God. I knew you would bring my children back to me." She pulls Brian closer and holds him tight for several minutes then backs up, holding his shoulders at arm's length. Grabbing her bag from the pew, she races through the doors and into the street, hailing a cab and leaving Brian standing in the aisle of the church.

A few minutes later, Zack enters the cathedral, looking for Anna Marie, according to the text she had sent him.

"Brian?" Zack sprints to him and throws his arms around his precious son. "Where have you been? Where's your mother?"

"She left..."

"What?" Zack interrupts. "You've been missing, and she leaves you! *How could she do that?*" He punches the air in his frustration.

"It's okay, Dad. I understand now."

"What do you mean?"

"I was in the most beautiful place, and Lexi was there, alive and well. But she's caught, Dad, between the two dimensions, because Mom won't let her go. Mom can't because she feels guilty. The guilt is so consuming that it blocks any light in her present life which includes you and me. It has stopped the gift that was supposed to come from her death. In this other dimension, Mom spared hundreds of families from the same hurt by giving Lexi's death a purpose. She created a hair band that would alert a parent if their child was under water for more than 15 seconds. She named it the 'Lexi Alert,' so then she could focus on all the lives Lexi saved instead of her guilt and anguish. We all have an amazing bond in the other dimension that brings us together, rather than one that pushes us apart."

Zack pulls his son into his chest, holding him close. A tear escapes and runs down his check. "Okay, let's go find your mom."

Zack and Brian find Anna Marie hunched over her daughter's body, sobbing. Her son has returned to her, but her daughter remains unchanged, in a place she can't reach.

"Mom..."

Anna Marie lifts her head to see her husband and son standing in the doorway. Her eyes are puffy and red from crying, her hair disheveled from her unsteady fingers raking through it.

"Go on, Brian. Tell your mom what you told me." Zack pats Brian gently on the back. Brian recounts his experiences, this time for his mother. Upon hearing his words, Anna Marie sobs once again, the wounds fresh and bleeding. Brian folds his mother into his arms.

"Mom, Lexi wanted me to tell you something. She wanted me to tell you it's time to let her go, and she asked me to do something for her. Close your eyes."

Anna Marie closes her eyes. Brian leans in close, rubbing his nose against hers. He whispers, "I love you, puppy."

Anna Marie slips from her chair, collapsing to the floor. Zack rushes over to her. Only Lexi would have known about their nighttime ritual. That was the only thing that was theirs, the only thing no one else knew about. The three of them remain entwined on the floor, finding comfort in each other's embrace.

"There's something else," Brian pulls away. His parents look at him expectantly. "She wants you to do it together. She says you made her together, and she wants you to let her go together. She says not to worry. Once you let her go, you will feel more of her joy all around you." Anna Marie and Zack turn to each other, staring deeply into each other's eyes. Anna Marie nods.

"Don't worry, Mama." Brian says. "We will see her again when it's our time to leave. We will all be together as one, I've experienced that connection on the other side.

Anna Marie pulls her son to her chest. "I love you, Brian. I'm so sorry I haven't been there for you. I hope you know how deep my love is for you."

"I know, Mom," he sighs as he welcomes his mother's comforting embrace.

"A new record has been reached today," Brad reports with a placid face. "Cigarettes and alcohol sales are at a record low today. Sales haven't fallen to this level since the days of prohibition. Despite the failing economy, Weight Watchers stock is up, charities are booming, and an amazing co-op program has been developed online. It is suspected that this sudden rise is in response to the recent special on the Oprah network. In national news, with the recent guilty verdict in the highly publicized trial of the regime leader charged with the kidnapping of Grace, the President has released a statement revealing that for the first time in the history of the United States, the execution will be shown live on television. Religious leaders are up in arms, as that is Good Friday, a holy day, and it should not be tainted with hate and vengeance. Furthermore, religious evangelists are prophesying that this is the beginning of the apocalypse. The execution is scheduled for Friday at 7:00 P.M. Stay tuned as we continue to bring you the latest regarding this controversial event."

Glued to the television, Christine knows what she needs to do. She can't let this happen; she has to convince the president not to go through with this terrible mistake. She picks up the phone resting on the end table and quickly calls Joanne to plot her attack. She knows that Simon is the only one from the *Times* who will have access to the viewing.

After several hours of brainstorming, she and Joanne develop a pretty elaborate plan. With the prowess of a clever thief, Christine puts her plan in motion. She picks up the phone and calls the one person who can make it all happen.

"Johnny, I need your help."

The darkness seeps into Kevin's apartment like the morning dew, slowly stealing away the light of day and replacing it with shadow; Kevin only reaches to turn on the lamp when he is surrounded by it. His eyes are weary, but sleep continues to fail him.

"Okay. Maybe Abba is on to something," Kevin mutters to the walls in his frustration. He walks over to Kate's desk, sitting at it for the first time since she disappeared. She said she needed it to pay bills and crunch numbers. Her papers still scatter the surface, untouched. He has tried a time or two to complete some of his course work there, but failed in the end and opted for the sofa.

Kevin lifts the papers gently in an effort to locate a blank page and a pen. Locating both, he stares at the stark white page as it returns the favor. He taps his pen absently on the wooden surface, the sound echoing in his ears. "What do I say, even if it is hypothetical?" Kevin whispers.

Kevin puts pen to paper.

To a brave soldier's parents,

My name is Kevin Thompson, and I looked into your son's eyes as he died. He was a young boy with great strength and courage. He had no fear; he was fighting for his country. You should be proud. In that moment of truth, as we stared down the barrel of each other's gun, your son was more of a man than I. He could have shot me first, but the compassion in him caused him to pause. It happens when the enemy suddenly has a face. That was his only shortcoming, and I know that where he has gone, he will be rewarded for such mercy.

I am so sorry that I took such a gift from you.

Kevin pauses to reread the words on paper. Tears stream down his face, and he lowers his head into his hands. In his suffocating desire for comfort, he can almost feel the arms of his wife wrap around him. He can almost smell her.

"Baby, don't cry."

At the sound of her voice, Kevin turns around to see Kate, a beautiful angel in the soft glow of lamplight. Unable to speak, he buries his face in her chest and releases years of hurt onto her printed dress. His sobs slowly subside, weakening into small jerks of his head and shoulders.

Leaning back, he takes a long look at his wife. "Kate..." He pulls her down into his lap, wrapping his arms around her waist. "You have no idea how much I need you." He buries himself once again into her comfort.

"Yes, I do."

He can hear the love in her voice as she holds him for the first time in months.

"Were you on the other side?"

"How did you know?"

"Someone else came back, before you."

"How many of us were there?" Kate strokes the back of his head.

"I think it was something like 30,000."

"That's awesome!"

"Huh?" Kevin straightens up to look Kate in the eye. "How can you say that?"

"When you go to the other side, you know how to do it right on this side. Some people already get it right, but most people need a little help. I know I did."

"I don't understand."

"The place I went to was a reality that had complete trust in the divine. When something difficult crossed your path, you didn't blame

God, because you knew that He would transform whatever pain had crossed your path into a lesson that would change you for the better. Your focus was on the gift from the experience rather than on the suffering. I think they called it Divine Alchemy."

"How did you get to the other side?"

"It was the strangest thing. I was looking into the mirror, crying and feeling helpless. Everything was going wrong with us, and I didn't know how to fix it. I looked at my reflection, but instead of seeing myself, I could only see my tears. I tried to wipe them away. The next thing I knew, I was suddenly looking back at myself from the other side of the mirror, kind of like Alice and the looking glass. I was living in two worlds simultaneously." Searching desperately through her vocabulary to find the words to convey her incredible experience, Kate tries again. "Like the superstring theory we learned about in college, that we live simultaneously in different dimensions at the same time. I somehow found a way into the subatomic world through the wave function of my tear. It's almost like these dimensions are fractals of each other but slightly different." Kate pauses. "I know this sounds so crazy; but I lived in a place where you were happy. We were happy."

"I believe you." Kevin touches the side of her face. "What was our life like?"

"Oh, Kevin, it was incredible." Kate's face grows wistful as she remembers the life that could have been. "You were happy, grateful, and really making a difference in young men's lives. You still went to war, and you still faced that boy; but when you returned, you started a service organization for young college men called 'Young Men with Guns.' Through this organization, you told your story; but partnered it with an outreach program to help young men who had become disabled from the war, as well as families who had lost their sons. The young men assisted them in physical projects, emotional support, and fundraising. You helped hundreds of young men understand what it means to enlist, what they were really agreeing to. There was no free lunch. The government would pay for your education, but you would repay them with service. That service just might lead you to a 12-year-old soldier and a choice. Not everyone has what it takes to be a soldier. It is reserved for those who have a special calling, not someone looking for free education."

"That's incredible," Kevin sighs in amazement as though this dimension had the ability to read his mind. "Since I've been sober, I've actually been lying awake at night, thinking about how I could help others — not make the same mistake, you know?"

"Thank God you stopped drinking." Kate grabs and hugs him even tighter. "Oh, I forgot the most amazing thing."

Kevin looks up, encouraging her to continue.

"I was pregnant, and not only had you remodeled our whole bathroom, but you also had started working on a nursery."

Kevin grabs her hand and leads her to the bathroom, which he had gutted and lovingly renovated tile by tile; hoping in his heart it was a premonition of the future to come: a healed marriage and the blessing of a longed-for child.

"There is someone here to see you, Dr. Windsor. No appointment, but she refuses to leave without speaking to you."

"Thanks, Patty. I have a minute before the next patient. Send her in." Laura sits behind her desk, shuffling papers and waiting for the unexpected visitor to enter.

"Dr. Windsor?" Ms. Thomas, Sarah's mother, pokes her head in the doorway.

"Please, Ms. Thomas, come in. Take a seat." Laura rises and motions to the empty chair in front of the desk.

"Oh, no, thanks. I'll just be a minute." Sarah's mom busies her hands with her hair. "I just want to thank you... for helping Sarah."

Those words float across the room and land gently in Laura's ear. Her body grows warm, and a smile forms across her face. At that moment, Laura realizes Sarah's mother loves her, but just doesn't know how to show it. "Well, Ms. Thomas, I'm just glad that I could be there at the right time. I hope everything improves for the two of you."

After leaving the office, without knowing exactly why, or what to expect, Laura drives out of the city to see her mother. Unsure of what to say, she raps on the door and then looks around. The neighborhood hasn't really changed all that much since the last time Laura stood on that doorstep. The trees are taller, the houses are older, and the sidewalks have a few more cracks and crevasses for an unsuspecting bicycle wheel.

Laura looks back at the door, anticipating it to open, but it still remains clamped shut. Accepting the fact that she has come for nothing, Laura turns to descend the set of stairs leading down to the street. Her foot dangles mid-step when she hears the distinct rattle of a doorknob. She turns back to find the silhouette of her mother in the doorway, backlit by her reading lamp in the living room.

"Hello?"

"Mother." Laura takes a step towards the door, more of her hitting the light cascading from the open doorway.

"Laura? My goodness. It's been a long time since I laid my eyes on you. Come in." Her mother steps back into the house, and heads to her recliner. Laura follows her, shutting the door behind her.

"Where's your husband?" Laura looks around for any trace of the man who molested her.

"Dead. Cancer took him a few years back." Her mother pulls out a cigarette from the pack on the end table and lights it.

"Oh." Silence fills the room. "I've been thinking about you a lot lately." Laura sits down on the sofa near her. "I had this patient a few months ago, a little girl, sweet as she could be; but her mom's boyfriend wasn't so nice... he did horrible things to her. Her mom wouldn't believe her. Kind of reminded me of someone..." Laura looks into her mother's eyes, waiting for some glimmer of recognition, of ownership.

"Oh, really? Who?" Her mother's vacant eyes meet her own.

"You, Mom," Laura replies in disbelief. After all of these years, her mother still doesn't believe her. "You still don't believe me. I am your daughter, and you don't believe me."

"I have no idea what you're talking about!" Her mother sits up straight in the recliner. The light from the reading lamp falls on her mother's face, showing Laura how old her mother has gotten. Her smooth face is now pitted and creviced from years of smoking and sun. Her jowls sag, creating the appearance of a feisty bulldog; but her eyes give her away. Laura finds sadness there, the sadness of years of loneliness. She recognizes it, because that used to be her, shutting people out. The hardness around Laura's heart softens, and in its place, pity resides. She finally realizes she doesn't need her mother's apology to extend forgiveness to her.

"I'm sorry I haven't been in touch, Mom." Laura places her hand on her mother's knee.

"I feel the same way, dear." She takes another drag on her cigarette then puts it out and grabs for Laura's hand. "I feel the same way."

The sun rises right on time, despite the gloom that seems to hover over the capital. An eerie quietness envelops the world, much like the skin-prickling calm before the harrowing winds of a tornado. To Christine, it feels as if even Mother Nature is expressing her displeasure with the ignorance of man. She anxiously waits in a nearby coffee shop for the fruits of her labor, her knee jittering uncontrollably and her fingers swirling the tea bag in her mug. Anytime now, Derek should be strolling in with the credentials she needs to get close to the president.

A few days ago, she was able to convince Johnny to call Derek James, a friend who works at the Washington Police Department. He owes Johnny a favor for help in a particularly personal case, so it didn't take too much convincing to get him on board. All Officer James has to do is detain Simon and confiscate his press passes, and if everything goes according to plan, Christine will have those passes any minute.

"Christine." Derek glides into the chair opposite Christine, easily identified by her condition, nine months and counting.

"Did you get it?" Christine jerks excitedly.

"Yes, so tell Johnny we are even." Derek slides the passes across the table, and Christine slips them into her purse. "Thank you!"

"No problem. I actually enjoyed detaining him. He really is as big of a jackass as Johnny said."

"You have no idea."

Derek laughs. "Well, I hope they help you. Johnny says you're trying to save the world."

"I'm going to try." Looking down at her watch, Christine realizes that she's late and hoists herself up from the booth. "Thanks again." Christine shakes Derek's hand and then turns around and disappears through the door of the diner.

Thanks to Joanne's resourcefulness, Christine's picture fits perfectly over the old picture of Simon as she reconfigures the pass while being jostled in the back of a cab. Finally, she places the string over her head watching it dangle from her neck and slides to the side, diverted by the perfect little beach ball belly beneath her shirt. At nine months pregnant, Christine doesn't fit the typical profile of a superhero, but one should never underestimate the fierce tenacity of an exhausted, cranky bundle of hormones. Christine exits the cab and totters across the parking lot, the best impression of a run she can manage.

When she arrives at the viewing, the crowd of people overwhelms her. She has to get closer. "Excuse me. Excuse me." Christine elbows her way through to the front, using her protruding baby to advance her progress. Finding herself near the podium, Christine plants her feet, refusing to move until the president enters to address the media.

Right on time, the President enters, approaches the podium, and begins to address the crowd. A hush trickles from the front of the room to the back, everyone straining to hear his profound words.

"Almost a year ago today, I came before you as the President, as an American, and as a father, and I announced the disappearance of our only child, Gracie." The President pauses, lowering his head in an attempt to compose himself. Clearing his throat, he begins again. "But

I am not alone in my suffering. I have each one of you as company. Since that time, thousands of Americans have also disappeared. These unspeakable acts of cruelty were attacks on the American people. As I said that day, and as I stand before you today, I say it again: We will not tolerate terrorist acts against the American people. We will fight back; without hesitation."

Applause breaks out among the journalists, and select audiences. Like the waving arms of cheering fans at a baseball game, shouts of approval ripple across Washington's great mall.

The audience quiets, anticipating his next words. He continues, "This is not just an attack against us as Americans. This is an attack against all people. People are afraid, I am afraid; afraid of losing a parent, a sibling, a child, a friend. There has been no discrimination, taking men, women, and even children of every color and creed. This execution, this choice, that I haven't made lightly, will send a very clear message. We will not tolerate, nor have we ever tolerated, terrorist attacks on the American people." To emphasize his point, the President slams his fist on the podium. The sound is muffled by another spontaneous eruption of applause. The President waits for silence to return before beginning again.

"There has been controversy surrounding the date of this execution. It is my regret that it has to occur on a holy day for most. However, wars do not cease for a holiday, and neither must we. We must always be vigilant, steadfast. America is built on the strength of her people and on her word, and the sentence must be carried out, whatever the consequence. We have only one choice: to look terror in the eye and eradicate it. We will not choose submission. We will protect the very essence of America, a free people who refuse to live in fear. With a profound sense of the solemn and even tragic character of the step I am about to take; and of the grave responsibilities that it involves; in unhesitating obedience to what I deem my constitutional duty, I will take the life of this transgressor against the American people, and for my daughter, Grace. While we perform this execution, this deeply momentous thing, let us be very clear, and make crystal clear to the entire world, what our motive and our objective are: that the United States of America will not be victimized. We are at the beginning of an age in which it will be insisted that the same standards of conduct and of responsibility for wrongdoings shall be observed among all nations. We will band together in zero tolerance."

The President surveys the room from behind the large oak podium, as the crowd once again fills the room with sounds of approval. Hands shoot up like grass after a rain, the voices buzzing like a disturbed hive.

Christine seizes her opportunity and begins waving her arms and shouting his name. "Mr. President! Mr. President!" Shoving through the crowd with her rotund belly as an aid, she screams incessantly, desperate to be heard.

From the interrogation room at the Washington airport, Simon watches the live feed from his cell phone. He shakes his head in disbelief when he notices Christine screaming like a lunatic at the President of the United States. From much further away, Hal is also shaking his head from his corner office in New York, thankful he fired her before she had completely lost her mind.

Taken aback by her flailing arms and hysterical screams, the President acknowledges Christine with a nod. "Yes?"

"Sir, what did your daughter say to you in your dream on 12/12/12? You woke up at 12:12, didn't you?"

The President's mouth opens in surprise. His eyes bulge at her unexplainable knowledge, and he is unable to speak.

Refusing to give up, Christine repeats the question. "What did she say to you?"

Unsure of how the words leave his empty brain and exit his mouth, he responds, "She told me to teach the world to love."

"Sir, is that all she said? What was the whole message?"

Stunned by her accuracy, he answers her again. "She told me to teach the world to love, and I would see her again."

"Forgive me sir, but are you doing what she asked?"

The President's face grows blank. He looks around the room at the puzzled faces.

Christine continues, "Sir, if you execute this man, you will never see your daughter again."

The President remains motionless for a moment, absorbing the words and processing them one by one. He raises two fingers of his right hand and motions for the Secretary of State to join him at his side. The President whispers into his ear, then turns and disappears behind those large familiar doors. Instantly, agents are on each side of Christine.

"Please come with us, ma'am." One of them gently grabs her by the elbow and maneuvers her through those same large doors and into a small room off the main hall. The President is waiting for her.

"How did you know that?" He paces back and forth in front of a large bookcase. He stops to look at Christine, waiting anxiously for an answer.

"I know because I had one, too."

"I don't understand." The President stops momentarily to glance at Christine, his brow furrowed with confusion and his eyes tired. He continues to pace.

"Mr. President, let me tell you a story."

For the third time, Christine recounts the journey of the group, their personal journeys of forgiveness and grace, ending with the return of their loved one. "You must show mercy. This man you are about to murder is guilty only of taking credit for God's work. He doesn't have your daughter, and only you can get her back. Let him go, and teach the world to forgive."

The President pauses for a brief moment, then shakes his head. "I cannot risk putting the American people in harm's way because three people and a dog came back with some crazy story." The President motions for the body guard to escort her out of the building.

"You're making a grave mistake, sir. If you do this — if you kill this man, then you may never see your daughter again."

Agents surround her on either side as the President exits the room and makes his way down the hallway.

"Sir, please!" Christine yells after him as the guards restrain her arms. She squirms beneath their firm grasp as they escort her down the main hall towards the Corral for safe keeping. "Oooo," Christine doubles over as a sharp pain originating in her abdomen shoots down her legs. Bracing her hands on her knees, she catches her breath.

"Ma'am, are you okay?" One of the agents touches Christine on the shoulder.

"Yeah. Yeah, I'm okay." Christine rolls herself back up, one vertebra at a time. Soft but determined footsteps echo through the large carpeted hallway, and as Christine straightens, she finds herself face to face with the First Lady.

"Tell me everything you know about my daughter."

Christine recounts the story, hitting the high points as they walk swiftly toward the large double doors. "I must tell you, if the President executes this man, you will never see your daughter again."

The First Lady's face flushes, fear and determination settling into every pore. As much as it pains Christine to be so tactless, she has done what she came to do: ignite a passion in the First Lady that no one would be able to stop.

"Stop the President now!" The First Lady shouts to the bodyguard, who in turns signals the others to stop him before he enters the assembly. But they are too late.

The President takes a deep breath and steps back into the pressroom, where an eager crowd waits an explanation. Stepping toward the podium, he is stopped by two Secret Service agents. "I'm sorry, sir. Your wife insists on seeing you." Confused, the President allows himself to be escorted back into the hallway and to his wife. Confusion turns to apprehension when he sees the look on his wife's face. He has seen that look only once before, and he rallies himself to stand his ground.

"You will not execute this man."

"I took an oath to protect this country, Carol. I can't just disregard that because some crazy pregnant woman shows up spouting the spiritual truths about life."

"And what about the oath you took to protect our love?"

"What are you saying, Carol?"

"I'm saying if you're wrong, and you execute this man and take my baby away from me forever, I will never forgive you."

"Don't do this to me, Carol. Not now." He rubs his temples, a scowl permanently attached to his face.

"No. You don't do this to me!" The iciness in her voice sends chills directly to his heart. "I have sacrificed everything for you – my dreams, my education, my passions, all for *you*; to stand beside *you*. What have you ever done for *me*? I have loved you through your childish bouts of anger and your addictive relationship with your work. I have stood beside you regardless of the pain it's cost me. And I am telling you now: if you kill this man, then you are sentencing our child and our marriage to the same fate."

Defeated, he hangs his head, and with heavy footsteps, the President walks back through the door of the pressroom yet again, approaching the podium. Confused as to what his next action should be, the President wrestles with the ultimatum from his wife and the seeds of doubt planted by Christine. In the deafening silence, he stands gripping the podium, the words of his daughter swimming in his head.

He could live with disappointing the American people. He has crossed that bridge before during his four years in office; but he couldn't live with making a decision that could take his daughter or his wife away from him forever. Frozen in front of the podium, he finally turns and walks to the handcuffed regime leader, waiting for his final moments. The President leans in close to his ear and, in a low voice, asks him one last time, "Do you know where my daughter is?" He searches his scraggly face for a clue, for a glimmer of acknowledgement. The prisoner, looking him in the eyes, responds, "On my soul, I do not know where she is."

The President nods his head with resolve. He steps behind and removes the handcuffs, releasing the prisoner. The prisoner drops to his knees in gratitude, praising Allah. The President helps him back to his feet, delivering him into the custody of the Secret Service.

The crowd of gathered reporters and political elite burst into chaotic shouts of frustration and anger, uncomprehending how the President could free the man responsible not only for his daughter's disappearance but for that of so many other Americans as well.

Aware of the aggressive crowd, the President turns to face them and attempts to speak. "I... I fear I have made..." The President raises his head to face the heckling crowd. Among the scowling faces in the crowd, something catches his eye. He squints, straining to see it clearer. Like an angel sent from heaven, he sees her way in the back, waving and smiling.

"Grace?" the President whispers, afraid to trust the vision before him. Their eyes meet. "Gracie!" He jumps down from the platform into the crowd, desperate to touch her, to hold her.

"Daddy! Daddy!"

The President fights through the crowd, as Grace runs straight for her daddy's welcoming arms.

"I knew I would see you again." She hugs her daddy's neck with all her might. "I missed you, Daddy! I love you so much!"

Unable to speak, he holds her tightly in his arms, hearing only her sweet voice in his ear as the reporters gather around them to snap a photo that will surely make the front page news. The First Lady bursts through the double doors and races to join them, eager to hold her daughter in her arms. Smiling, Gracie wraps her arms around her family, kissing and hugging them both as tight as she can. The First Lady is overcome with joy as the loves of her life are reunited. Their eyes catch, and she mouths to her husband, "Thank you."

"You wanted to see me?" Christine meekly enters Hal's office.

"I did. Please sit down." Hal motions for her to sit in the chair opposite his desk. Christine obeys. "I was going to prosecute you for your little stunt on Friday, stealing credentials, false representation – I could go on."

Christine swallows hard.

"As it is, I got a phone call this morning from the President of the United States. He wanted to know how to get hold of you. Not sure why he needed to find out from me, with the CIA and FBI at his disposal, except to make sure I gave you your job back."

Christine's face glows as she jumps up to hug him. "Thank you, thank you, thank you! You won't regret this, Hal."

"Make sure that I don't." Hal snaps, "Now get off me."

Christine sits back down in her chair. "Actually, I also got a call from the President this morning. He and the First Lady want to thank me by having me for a private dinner at the White House. We thought it would be best to wait until after the baby comes. Oooo!" Christine jerks and grabs her belly.

"What?"

"I'm not sure but it's been happening all morning." Christine's brow furrows. "Ooohh. I think they're contractions."

"Oh, no you don't. You already puked in my office. No more bodily functions in ...."

"Ummm...," Christine interjects. "Sorry."

Hal looks over the desk at Christine and notices a puddle of water underneath her chair. She slips to the end of her chair to try to stand up, but Hal stops her.

"Oh, hell, Christine. For God's sake, sit down."

If Christine hadn't been doubled over in pain, she would have smiled at Hal's unusual concern for her, his prized reporter, hand-picked and personally groomed by him. As it is, Hal's unorthodox compassion goes unnoticed.

"And keep that baby in place until I get the paramedics here." Hal darts behind his desk for the phone and begins dialing.

"Hal, I can't wait. You are going to have to drive me."

"What? Isn't there someone else?"

Christine screams through another contraction, "Hhhaaaaaaaaal!"

"Ok, ok. But we're taking your car!" Hal darts back to Christine to help her out of the chair.

"Hand me my purse. I need my phone."

"You want to make a call now?"

"Just give me the purse," Christine snarls through gritted teeth. She digs for her cell phone and dials Johnny. "It's time. Where are you? No, there's no time for that. I'll be fine. Okay, I'll wait for the escort. Just hurry." Christine throws the phone into her bag.

With her arm over his shoulder for support, Christine and Hal make slow progress to the elevator and into the parking deck. They make it to her car, and Hal tries his best to help her into the passenger seat. Joanne, just arriving, notices Hal and Christine.

"Oh, my God, it's time!" she shouts.

Hal looks up when he hears Joanne's voice. "Thank God! Get over here. You're driving!" Joanne quickly gets into the driver's seat. "Besides, I'm not good with all this baby stuff. I'll send flowers." He slams the car door as Christine squirms on the other side of the door.

"I've got this," Joanne replies confidently, and then the parking garage is filled with the sound of squealing tires as she guns it out onto the street and right behind the motorcycle police escort that Johnny has sent. The perfection in timing makes it appear as though everything is being orchestrated by God himself, making Christine more relaxed in knowing that it will all turn out just fine.

———— • ————

Laura has already been called, and is ready and waiting when Christine arrives. "You are going to do great, Christine. Let's go have a baby!" The head nurse wheels Christine into the delivery room and gets her into a hospital gown. As she helps Christine into the bed, Laura remembers something, something she has forgotten until that moment.

"Christine, I just remembered the most wonderful dream I had last night. You had your baby, and it was a boy."

"Huh! That's funny — exactly what my mom said." Christine grips the rails of the delivery bed as another contraction hits. "I don't care what it is; *just get this baby out of me!*"

And that is exactly what she does. Eight hours later, Laura hands Christine a beautiful baby boy. Johnny has missed it by five minutes. He would have made it on time, but the train was late.

"I didn't know if I should bring you flowers or balloons, so I just brought you what every girl wants." Johnny steps aside to clear the doorway. "Her mom."

Christine's mom comes around the corner of the door.

"Oh, my God. I am so glad that you are both here. Come here!" Christine motions for them to come see the sleeping baby. The little bundle of life in her ams instantly mesmerizes them. "Meet little Anthony."

Tears immediately stream down her mother's face. "You named him after your father?" Unable to speak further, she reaches out to hold her one and only grandson.

Epilogue

Three weeks have passed since the excitement of Anthony's birth and the miraculous return of the President's daughter Grace. After such a disruption, Christine is finally falling into the rhythm of her life with the baby, the new light of her life. While on a walk in the early morning, Christine is suddenly overwhelmed with the need to see Jesse, to thank him for teaching her how to nurture herself, resulting in this amazing little being. Christine piles Anthony into the car and takes a relaxing drive out to Jesse's office in Mamaroneck .

She notices an unusual vacant feeling to the building as she miraculously finds a parking space right in front of his office. The building is unlocked, so Christine carefully opens the door and walks hesitantly into the vacant building, with little Anthony strapped on the front of her. Luckily, the elevator is still operating, and Christine takes it up to the fifth floor, where the group has met every Thursday for the past seven months. As she exits the elevator, she immediately sees a "for rent" sign hanging on the door, with an agent's number listed below it. Christine scrambles for her cell phone hiding deep in her bag. Confused, she dials the displayed number and waits for the agent to answer on the other end of the invisible thread.

"Yes. I was wondering about the forwarding information for the tenant who rented the office space on the fifth floor. Would you be able to help me?"

The agent exhales a scruffy laugh. "That space has been empty for the last two years. Know anyone interested in renting it?"

"Two years? Are you sure? I am talking about the office space at 419 West End on the *fifth* floor. I was just there a few weeks ago. Dr. Abba rented this space."

"Look, lady, I clean that space, and I'm telling you nobody has been there."

Christine's face grows red with frustration, and before he can finish repeating himself, she hangs up the phone. The reporter in her is unwilling to accept the crass man's explanation, and she walks over to the door and tests the knob under her hand. It gives in and swings open, revealing falling plaster in a dusty room. "Guess he hasn't cleaned this space in a while, huh, little Anthony?"

An oversized wooden desk standing in the center of the room is the only piece of furniture remaining.

Her brow furrows with disbelief and confusion. There are no remnants of the lonely plant in the corner or the tattered mismatched chairs and sofa. Everything that made this office so familiar and comforting is gone. She starts to jostle Anthony as he begins to fuss, soothing him with her voice. She walks over to the desk and finds an envelope on it, with "Christine" written across the middle.

Christine looks around her before snatching it up, almost expecting someone to appear. She slides her finger across, breaking the seal. The paper slides out easily, and Christine unfolds it and begins to read.

Christine,

Remember, it is when you allow yourself to slow down, giving God your attention daily that you can begin to experience Grace. It is the trust in Divine Alchemy that no matter what darkness is presently consuming your existence, God can transform your sorrows and assist you in embracing joy, yet again. It is the opening of your heart to receive that gift of grace without any doubt, fear, anxiety, or presumed disappointment, that unlocks or shifts you into the Lost Paradigm ~ Heaven on Earth. Keep in mind that people shift between paradigms through vibrations and emotions, so the thoughts that occupy your mind will also dictate the paradigm in which you will live.

Know that God is omnipotent, meaning he can transpire his being in the word and the word in him. So when you speak his name, he is with you. Do this daily. The real mastery is learning to become, not only more aware of the Divine, but to also sustain connection and co-creation with God by shifting from a dark and fearful thought paradigm to a loving and grateful thought paradigm. Tell the others that by choosing to shift their thoughts from guilt, fear, anger, and shame to embracing grace, love, blessing and gratitude, they are now co-creating a paradigm very similar to the one that their missing loved ones shared with them. Teach the world how to do this, and you will see me again.

With Love, Blessing, & Gratitude,

Jesse Abba

"GOD has done all this, so that we seek him,
draw near to him and [experience JOY] through him." Acts 17:27